13 Canadian Ghost Stories

13 Canadian Ghost Stories

Edited by Ted Stone

Western Producer Prairie Books
Saskatoon, Saskatchewan

Western Producer Prairie Books
Saskatoon, Saskatchewan

Cover illustration and design by Warren Clark/GDL

Printed and bound in Canada

The publisher acknowledges the support received for this publication from the Canada Council.

Western Producer Prairie Books is a unique publishing venture located in the middle of western Canada and owned by a group of prairie farmers who are members of Saskatchewan Wheat Pool. From the first book in 1954, a reprint of a serial originally carried in the weekly newspaper *The Western Producer*, to the book before you now, the tradition of providing enjoyable and informative reading for all Canadians is continued.

Canadian Cataloguing in Publication Data

Main entry under title:

Thirteen Canadian ghost stories

ISBN 0-88833-272-6

1. Ghost stories, Canadian (English).* I. Stone, Ted, 1947-

PS8237.G5T44 1988 C813'.0872 C88-098089-3
PR9197.32.T44 1988

Contents

Introduction

The stories in this book are, in many ways, uncommon ghost stories. One is about a ghost who is haunted by humans. Another, about a ghost who only manifests himself through a piece of antique furniture. A third, about a disgraced athlete who comes back from the dead to play baseball in an Iowa farmyard. Some of the ghosts in these stories even do good deeds.

Canada, to a reader of traditional European ghost stories, might seem an inhospitable place for ghosts. We have no decayed and crumbling castles, no bloodthirsty noblemen in our history. Ghost stories are here, though. The folklore of every region of the country is rife with tales about spirits and hauntings.

Ghost ships still sail the Great Lakes. Fiery schooners visit the waters of the Maritimes. Spirits continue to haunt the old lumber camps of the north woods and protect ancient Indian burial grounds on the Prairies. They hike the mountains of the West and ride canoes and dog sleds in the territories. And in the dark of quiet summer nights, their tales are told around campfires from Newfoundland to Vancouver Island.

When I first began thinking about Canadian ghosts, I thought about these ghosts, the ghosts we've learned about in campfire stories and traditional oral tales, not the literary ghosts of books and magazines. Almost everyone I've talked to about ghosts has had a story of some kind, or at least part of a story. Since I began this project, friends have told me about old houses with lights that come on by themselves, doors or windows that open and close of their own accord, and sounds in the night that come from no discernible earthly source.

Some of the most striking stories are local variations of tales commonly classed as urban or contemporary folklore. They're stories like the one of the hitchhiker who vanishes after being given a ride to her home. Confused, the driver of the car knocks at the door of the house and learns from the old couple who live there that his passenger was their daughter, a daughter who was killed in a highway crash seven years before and has been trying ever since to find a ride home.

Usually, in stories like this one, the teller of the tale is at least two or three people removed from any of the story's participants. They're stories that happened to the friend of a friend in another town. An acquaintance of mine told me once about listening to a radio call-in show in Halifax. One caller said that one day, just after her new neighbours had moved in, she heard a loud crash next door. She ran out to see what had happened and discovered a teenage boy lying by his car in the driveway. The boy was all right, but the car had slipped off the jack and fallen to the pavement.

As he got up, the boy explained that he had been under the car, working on the engine, when the jack gave way. As the car began to fall, someone grabbed his feet and pulled him to safety. The boy looked up to see a stranger only a couple of years older than himself. Then, in the moment it took for him to glance back at his car, the stranger disappeared. From the description the boy gave of his rescuer, the woman recognized her son, who had been killed ten years earlier when a jack had slipped and a car had crushed him.

We've all heard stories like these. They're stories that leave us, believers and skeptics alike, with chills running down our spines. You don't have to believe in ghosts to be afraid of them. You don't have to be interested in the occult or the macabre to fall under the power of a good ghost story.

Of all the stories in Canadian folklore, my favourites are the aboriginal legends. Many of the other folktales we call ghost stories are only anecdotes, partial tales, glimpses in the night. The stories in Native Canadian ghost lore, though, seem more complete.

Ironically, these traditional tales, stemming from an oral culture, seem to me the most nearly literary of our folktales about ghosts. They're more than sketchy recollections of seeing a phantom ship or coming across a spectre on a dark country road. In Native legends, the story is more important than the details, meaning comes from more than plot, and something else always happens than simply stumbling across an apparition.

A brief example can be found in the legend of the Qu'Appelle Valley in Saskatchewan. Perhaps the story came about because someone heard noises on the river. In the legend, though, the noises are of little importance. The real story is the explanation for them.

One night an Indian brave was travelling the river in a birch canoe. Suddenly, in the stillness, he thought he heard someone call his name. Frightened, he asked, "Who calls?" There was no reply, but soon he heard his name called again. Once more he responded with "Who calls?"

Again no one answered, but the next day when the young brave returned to his village, he learned that his fiancée had become sick. She had died the night before. He remembered the voice he had heard on the river and asked if she had called his name. Yes, the people told him, twice. Heartbroken, the young brave returned to his canoe and disappeared down the river. He was never seen again, but ever since, people travelling the Qu'Appelle occasionally hear the words "Who calls?" echoing through the valley.

It was because of ghost stories like this one and other Native legends that I renewed an interest in literary ghost stories, stories created by individual authors instead of taken from folklore. I had only been an occasional reader of ghost stories before, but I went back to them looking for stories as captivating as the Native legends.

Along the way, I discovered that Canadian writers, too, have had things to say about departed souls. Not surprisingly, I found that I felt more affinity for many of their tales than the traditional European ghost stories I had been reading. Spirits don't have to live in dungeons or rattle chains or haunt houses in the stereotypical manner of nineteenth-century ghost literature. Ghosts are just as likely to haunt an empty cabin in the Arctic or a modern hospital as an English manor house or European castle.

In this book, I've collected thirteen Canadian ghost stories that I've enjoyed reading and believe other people might enjoy as well. Some of the stories are from folklore. Most are from the authors' imaginations. I haven't selected the stories with any thought to regional representation or because they are of any particular style. The tales range from Native legends to parody, but the reason they are included here is that all of them are good stories.

Father Maurice Metayer's "The Ghost Hunter" is taken directly from the folklore of an Inuit people known as Copper Eskimos who live along Canada's mainland Arctic coast and the islands just to the north. Christie Harris's "Ghost Story" is a recounting of a West Coast Indian tale. Two other stories in this collection, Harry Paddon's "The Phantom Dog Team" and Julia Seton's "The Mackenzie River Ghost" are taken from the lore of particular regions of the country.

Seton's story offers an example of how well travelled these tales become. A strikingly similar account, though with different participants, was written by the fur trader Roderick MacFarlane in 1883 and published in the December, 1986 issue of the magazine *The Beaver.*

Will Bird's "Ghosts Have Warm Hands," like Paddon's "Phantom Dog Team" and Seton's "Mackenzie River Ghost," is recounted as fact. The remaining stories are completely fictional, but they range from Farley Mowat's "The Snow Walker," told in the straightforward manner of recollection, to W. P. Kinsella's fantasy "Shoeless Joe Jackson Comes to Iowa." "Shoeless Joe," like Mavis Gallant's "Up North" and H. R. Percy's "The Timeless Island," goes beyond what is conventionally thought of as a ghost story. These tales are individual hauntings of history, of heritage, of the mind.

Robin Skelton's "Householder" and Johann Polberg's "Kismet," on the other hand, seem more typically in the ghost story tradition. But each offers something more. Skelton's ironic conclusion and Polberg's benevolent innocence make each story distinctive. While Stephen Leacock's "Buggam Grange: A Good Old Ghost Story" parodies the traditional ghost story, Robertson Davies's "Conversations With the Little Table" manages to tell a real one while still maintaining Leacock's lightheartedness.

I've called these tales Canadian stories because they were written, with one exception, by Canadian authors. The exception, Julia Seton, recounts a story that happened in this country as told to her by her husband, Ernest Thompson Seton. Four stories, though written by Canadians, take place in other lands.

I thank Dee Barber, Father Felix Vallee, Rob Sanders, Colleen Odegard, and the staff at the Winnipeg Centennial Library for their help on this project. I also thank my wife, Patricia Pidlaski, for her wise counsel during the time this book took shape.

Householder

Robin Skelton

At first I didn't believe the house was haunted. I'd lived in it so long that I couldn't credit it. After all, what could it be haunted by? It wasn't very old; I myself was only the second owner and my predecessor had been very nondescript, a single man, like myself, with no tales of insanity, mania, sudden death or even mild unhappiness attached to his name. He'd died at around seventy-eight in hospital of something unimpressive like creeping heart disease, and I'd bought it a month or so after the estate had been settled. The house, too, had nothing unusual about it. It was more a cottage than a house, really, a living room and kitchen downstairs, two bedrooms upstairs, a tiny attic-cum-boxroom, and no basement. I suppose the garden might be considered a feature; it was unusually large for the size of the house, mostly shrubbery, and didn't require any attention at all—which was the way I liked it, engrossed in my own studies as I was. I wondered at first if my studies weren't responsible for the hauntings. I had spent a lot of time concentrating on the crystal ball, and, after all, it was possible that I had somehow welcomed in some spirit or energy that I hadn't planned on having as a guest. But then I dismissed this. I'm sure I would have known if anything like that had occurred. There would have been some sign. As it was, the haunting, which, as I say, I didn't at first credit, came as a complete surprise.

It was around Halloween that it happened. I'd just come down from the attic where I kept my crystal ball on a little table–it seemed so much more convenient to have it there, rather than be obliged to tidy it away every time I'd finished consulting it, in case a visitor or maybe one of the neighbourhood kids, who were always coming around and pressing their beastly squashed white noses to the window, should see it and jump to idiotic conclusions–when I sensed a presence in the living room. At first it was only a very dim sense of something, a sort of apprehension of a shape, but, as I moved downstairs towards it, it became more distinct and I actually saw it. It wasn't very definite; it was like a patch of flickering light about as tall as the average person, and the light had touches of colour in it as if in the centre there might be some kind of clothing, a dress or a blouse perhaps. I felt straight away that it was a woman.

Well, you can imagine my feelings. I was very disturbed, but also excited. I'd never had any kind of visitant before, though I had seen faces and shapes in the crystal ball a hundred times. I tried not to alarm the apparition. In fact, I sat quietly on the stair, watching it, and tried to 'tune in', to pick up its vibrations. After a while the light, which moved steadily around the living room as if it were inspecting it, altered a little in quality and I could see a sort of whitey-blue aura round it. It wasn't the first aura I'd seen, of course, but it was one of the first I'd registered at all strongly. I was fascinated. After a while it disappeared into the kitchen, and I crept down the stairs and followed it. I was working hard on becoming receptive. I tried to open myself to names. I didn't so much think or speculate, you understand, as let my mind wander freely waiting for a name. I was in the kitchen doorway, peering round to find what she was up to, when it came to me, quite suddenly, but with the utmost certainty. 'Anna,' I told myself. I must have said it aloud and frightened the creature for suddenly the energy field, or the spectre, or whatever you want to call it, was invisible. It didn't go away. I could still sense its presence. It just slipped into invisibility. Realizing that I had been clumsy I went back to my vantage point on the stairs and waited. Surely, if I were patient, she would appear again. I tried not to think about her in case that made her feel I was invading her privacy, but I got, in spite of my intention, a strong feeling of her age and situation. She was young, but not very young, and she was alone in the world. I thought (but this was more like guesswork and I wasn't too certain about it), that she might have been unhappily married at some time. I wondered if she had killed herself or been killed. I supposed it had to be one or the other, for why should she be wandering like this? I'd never heard, though, of a ghost actually moving in on a house, unless it had lived or died there or had memories of it, and I couldn't understand the situation at all. She might, I thought, have been a daughter or possibly a sister of the first owner and have returned here after death for some reason. I was most confused, and, I must admit, extremely stimulated.

I don't know how long I sat waiting on the stairs, but after a while I became aware of her moving towards me. At first it was only a sense of something approaching, and then, very faintly, I saw the light take shape. It was at the foot of the stairs and clearly intending to climb them. I thought it best to get out of the way and moved ahead of her onto the tiny landing. She paused within about a foot of me. I kept very still. Then she went into the main bedroom. I was a little embarrassed by this. Tidiness is not one of my virtues and I wished I had known that this was going to happen. I held my ground, however, and after a while she moved on to the other bedroom, and then descended the stairs. I was pleased that she hadn't gone up into the attic, though, after all, unless she was a very clever spirit she would not have known that there was anything up there other than the roof space. The stepladder that gave access to the trapdoor in the ceiling was leaning so casually against the wall that nobody would have suspected its function. I had no idea why I didn't want her in the attic. There wasn't a great deal there, only my little table with its black cloth and my crystal ball, and the stool I sat on, and my small collection of books. I wondered if ghosts knew about crystal balls; it seemed logical that they should, as these were used to communicate with them; on the other hand do any of us fully understand the workings of the telephone?

I was left with these reflections and doubts as she went back down the stairs and I sensed rather than saw her leave the house. After pacing up and down a good deal trying to come to terms with my perplexity, I myself went up into the attic and uncovered the ball and gazed into it. At first I could see nothing. Then I saw a little white smoke, which turned grey, and then blue, and then through the blue I saw a face emerging. I couldn't be certain that it was my visitor, but I felt that it might be her. She had brown hair, blue eyes and a rather determined jaw, and she was saying something to someone out of the picture. I couldn't actually hear words, but I got the gist of it. She had come to a decision, a quite definite decision. There was no doubt about it. Her lips moved and I wished I had been better at lip-reading. All I could guess at were the words 'will' and 'have'. Mercifully she said the same thing again and I interpreted her words as '. . . will have it' . . . or maybe 'with half it'. As I say, I was not good at lip-reading.

However bad I was at lip-reading, I was not without some deductive powers and began putting two and two together. She had clearly been inspecting the house. She had explored all the rooms. And then she had arrived at a decision. She had decided to move in. Therefore the words had been 'I will have it' though whom she was addressing I could not imagine. Maybe there are houseagents for ghosts? I giggled at the thought, a little hysterically I expect, for I was somewhat overwrought.

About a week later as I was wandering around upstairs thinking of nothing in particular I felt it happen. It was quite frightening, actually. There were rumbles everywhere around the house, and a great many blurred almost invisible shapes seemed to be moving everywhere. My furniture slowly took on a disturbing character, as if it were being superseded. There were shadows upon it. My little old footstool, a present from

India, darkened. The carpet, on the other hand, seemed brighter in places. The curtains even altered. I did not know what to do. This was no ordinary haunting. This was invasion. A whole conflux of spectral presences had moved in. I began to regret my work with the ball and my interest in the occult generally. I'd obviously opened the door to forces beyond my control. I thought of scattering salt on the stairs, but the salt was in the kitchen, and that was fully occupied by Them. I tried to think of an incantation of banishment, but the words would not come to me and, in any case, in magic as in everything else, I have always been an opponent of violence. At last I decided I would simply retreat until the situation had settled down and went into the garden to think the thing through. Try as I might, however, I could not understand what was going on. There seemed to be no precedent for it. I was victim of something previously unheard of. And yet the word 'victim' seemed inappropriate. I did not, I suddenly realized, feel particularly threatened. The presences were not malign. Indeed, I told myself, I was fortunate. I had been privileged to witness a previously unknown activity of the spirit world. I squared my shoulders, promising myself that I would keep meticulous notes for an article in one of the journals of parapsychology. Quite possibly my little house would become as famous as Borley Rectory.

I don't think I'd been in the garden more than an hour or so when I sensed that the house had grown quiet again. I went back inside and, sure enough, the disturbances, the rumblings, the busy movements had ceased. There was one presence remaining, however, a quiet, even weary one. I sensed it in the living room and very tentatively opened my mind to it. It was, as I had suspected, the lady spectre, Anna, and, as I sensitized myself further, I saw that her aura was now dull brown, signifying exhaustion. I wanted to speak to her, to convey to her that she was a welcome guest, but did not quite know how to contrive it. I did not like to go too close in case she would vanish. I thought it best to sit down quietly and wait upon events. We both sat there for quite a time, and I suppose that I must have dozed off. When I awoke it was quite dark, and she was nowhere to be seen. I did not even sense her presence in the kitchen where I made myself my usual cocoa, and noticed only that the cupboards seemed to have changed colour a little; there were odd shadows in them. Wearily, my mind entirely blank, I went upstairs. I was too tired to think of anything but bed. Indeed I was already half asleep when I got to the bedroom. I wondered a little about the ghost but decided that ghosts, like mortals, may need to sleep. Perhaps she had switched off for the night as it were. I yawned hugely and rolled into bed. At first it was comfortable, warm, welcoming and then, quite suddenly, it was fiercely cold, terrifyingly so, and I sat up, astonished, and the chill was all over me and the room was filled with alarm. Something in the room, even perhaps the room itself, was terrified. I felt, rather than heard, screams and sobs and leapt from bed in a panic. As I reached the landing I heard a tremendous bang as if the front door had been opened and slammed suddenly shut, and the whole house shook. Then a calm came upon me. The cold had gone, and I told myself that I really should expect this sort of thing, and maybe tonight I should be sensible and sleep in the spare room, in case the disturbance was still located in the main bedroom, and I turned in.

In the morning the house was still calm and, rather to my disappointment, the ghost appeared to have left, though there were odd shadows and colours still lingering in the living room, and some of the pictures on the walls had a strange look to them, as if they were covered with mist. After breakfast I decided that it was now over, that I had witnessed a temporary possession of the house, and that the after-effects – the shadows and the like – would dissolve over the next day or two. I was, quite honestly, disappointed, and after breakfast I went up to the attic to consult the crystal ball.

It took a little while for the ball to do anything but swirl with mist, but then the mist became smoke and the smoke became red and through the redness I saw, once again, a face. It was Anna. She was staring directly into my eyes, and her expression was angry. She was mouthing something, but this time I did not attempt a lip-reading. I was too upset. After all, what had I done wrong? I hadn't done anything. She could hardly blame me for being frightened the previous night–indeed it wasn't me that had been frightened–it was fright itself that had taken over the room. Probably it had something to do with her own guilt, I told myself, placing the cloth back over the ball. I thought I'd try another consultation when she'd had time to cool down. It's funny that I thought of her like that, as if she were a cross young woman who would get over her tantrums, not as if she were a ghost at all.

I spent the rest of the day pottering about. A small boy pressed his nose to the kitchen window once and I knocked on the pane and he ran away. Otherwise the day was uneventful. It wasn't until dusk that anything happened to suggest that this was not to be one of the usual humdrum days of my rather humdrum life. My first hint was my realization that Anna was back and not alone. I glimpsed her first in the drawing room, a vague shape in misty light, not red now, but more a sort of purple. I wasn't too pleased. She felt formidable. She was not, however, as formidable as the second presence. I couldn't see any shape to him at first, though I knew it was a him. He was quite formless but somehow very strong. There were all sorts of colours there. He made me nervous and I would have retreated to the garden again but I found myself prevented from doing so in some curious fashion. I wanted both to go and to remain. I was, as you may say, torn. It was an odd feeling, as if my will were not entirely my own, and I tried to retrieve my independence by reciting some of the conjurations I'd studied, but they had no effect, probably because the words came out a little jumbled, and I was nervous.

I hovered around for a while watching the two vague shapes shift, blur and flicker and wondered what to do. I seemed to have lost the power of decision, not surprisingly, I suppose. The circumstances were novel, to put it mildly, and I could think of nothing in my reading that would help. Exorcism, of course, occurred to me, but it seemed a little extreme and, in any case, I had never had occasion to try it out and was a bit vague as to the exact procedure. I knew that candles were involved, and salt and oil, but after that I was very insecure as to details and if I made a mistake I felt unhappily convinced that I would end up in trouble. Not knowing what to do, I decided I would merely sit around and make notes. After all, a first-hand account of even a minor haunting would interest an editor, and I was in a position to give a blow-by-blow account. However, upon starting my notes, I found it difficult to say exactly what was going on. The spectres, Anna and the Man – I did not sense his name though I tried – seemed to be moving all round the house, but in different directions, as if they were intent upon examining all the doors and windows and even all the walls. Like engineers, I thought – maybe they're checking the building for flaws, though they really had no need. It was sound as a bell. I followed Anna for a while, but then gave up. There was really nothing much to see. I decided, therefore, that I'd slip up into the attic and try the crystal ball again, but the trapdoor was stuck. It had been a bit damp during October so I blamed it on the weather. Or at least I pretended to blame it on the weather. I was becoming uneasy. It was as if the ghosts had taken over not only the house but my own life as well. I wondered if praying would do any good and knelt down on the landing underneath the trapdoor, but all I could remember was 'Gentle Jesus Meek and Mild', and it didn't seem appropriate. I'd never been a churchgoer, at least not since childhood.

It was at this stage that I began to feel resentful. What right had they to come into my home and occupy it in this fashion? What were their reasons? Who had made this the necessary meeting place for a couple of fidgety interfering spooks? I got really quite cross and decided I would tackle the pair of them head on. I went down the stairs in a rush, knocking over something or other, I don't know what, I just heard the clang at the foot of the stairs and didn't stop to enquire. I charged right on into the living room, and saw them both together in front of the fireplace. I intended shouting but the words didn't come. They were brighter than before and between the pair of them there was another sort of shape, a dark patch that was also bright, if I may be allowed a paradox. It flickered like a flame but it was black, a sort of black fire, that was also a hole, as if there were a rent in the fabric of things. I've never been hypnotized but at that moment I felt, I am sure, just as hypnotized people must feel; I was held by someone's will, and was both asleep and awake, and I was being drawn in towards the black flickering gap in the universe, for that is what I now felt it to be. I was terrified, of course, and yet I was observing my terror, as if I knew it would pass, almost as if I were standing over myself in fever, being both doctor and patient, at the time of crisis, at once delirious and coolly confident, at once panic-striken and relieved. This was the worst, but it was almost over; this was failure but also success.

I do not know what was being said but I heard words, or rather sensed the energy of words as I moved towards that darkness, trying simultaneously to hold myself back and yet to enter it, and then, quite clearly, I heard the command 'Go.' I didn't hear the word, of course, I just got the message. For a second I was appalled and also derisive. Who did they think they were to send me packing from my own house? How the devil could ghosts do this to anyone? I remembered stories of ghosts sending people screaming from midnight houses, their hair suddenly white, their reason gone, and I wondered if I was going to lose my mind. I thought not. I still seemed able to reason. It was merely my will power that had vanished. As I got closer to the dark it grew larger and at last I found myself able to speak. 'No!' I cried, 'No, *no*!' but it was useless. I was being evicted firmly, surely, but not without kindness. There was resentment but no terror, and then the resentment went and the darkness was round me and I closed my eyes and thought I was going to faint, but I didn't. All that happened was that the darkness became quite suddenly very bright indeed and I had the strange sensation of being, how can I put it, altered. Just for a moment I saw the faces of the ghosts clearly, the woman Anna and the Man; the faces were relaxed but stern; they had authority; they were to be obeyed. There was no choice. And maybe they were right. After all, I had lived in the house alone for a long time, and life had become a little tedious, a little humdrum. Maybe I should have moved out earlier, kept up with my friends more, travelled, even sought out those members of my family that I had not thought about for years. Outside the house I felt suddenly free. The house wasn't important any more. I spent a little time in the shrubbery wondering where to go, but it didn't seem to matter, and after a while the shrubbery faded and the house too and it was as if I were waking slowly and peacefully from a dream, or from an anaesthetic and, well, here I am, you see. Try rubbing the crystal ball with the silk a little and you'll see me more clearly and hear better. I always did that and it helped a lot. Of course, in those days, like you, I was probably a bit too intense and anxious about it and that always blurs the vision. It's a lot easier now that I'm more relaxed and not alone any longer, but, you know, I'm still surprised that a ghost could alter a man's life so thoroughly, and after so many years.

The Phantom Dog Team

Harry Paddon

All sparsely populated back country areas have their ghosts and Labrador, like the rest, has its share. The nice thing about the ghosts of Labrador is that they have kept the qualities of the old-timers of the era in which they entered the spirit world. They are a friendly, helpful group of spirits with more constructive things to do than merely to haunt the living as their more highly civilized counterparts seem to do. Instead, they appear to have a protective attitude towards their still living neighbors and descendants.

Such a one is the "Smoker" who, many times, has stuck his ethereal nose into the battering blasts of a Labrador blizzard to rescue a careless or unlucky traveller who should have known better.

How the Smoker got his name I couldn't say unless it derives from his ability to appear and vanish like a puff of smoke, or possibly it came from the fact that his appearance always occurred on a night of smoking thick drift on the barren lands he ranged. There is no question that the many to whom he appeared, including a newly-arrived and hard-boiled Hudson's Bay man who had never heard of him, firmly believe that he did indeed come to their aid and that without his help they would surely have perished. The particular incident I wish to relate occurred some 50 years ago and, since the people involved were friends of my family, I shall take a few liberties with their names though the story shall remain theirs as they told it.

Bill and Jane Gordon's winter home lay several miles inland from their summer fishing place at Bluff Head. Chosen for the generous area of woods that had furnished logs for the comfortable house and now sheltered it from the savage winds off the rocky barrens, the winter place was an isolated spot. The nearest neighbors were two families at Rocky Cove, 15 miles across the barren, rocky neck, and it was nearly 40 miles to the trading post at Rigolet. The Neck was something to be treated with respect by winter travellers, for the way across the bare, windswept ridges was unmarked and to go astray in one of the frequent winter gales was to risk death by freezing on its pitiless miles of shelterless rocks and ice, or by plunging storm-blinded from one of its many cliffs.

A few days before Christmas Bill and Jane left home to go to Rigolet to trade their furs and bring home a few extras from the store. The two children, 12-year-old Joe and little Janet, 10, were undismayed at the prospect of being left to fend for themselves for a night or two. Joe had considered himself a man for quite some time, for he could do a man's work in the woods or the fish stage, and he had been hunting and trapping alone for a couple of winters. Janet reckoned she could look after the house as well as any woman. Joe, as he helped his father harness the dogs that morning, was rather looking forward to being the boss for a while, and it was with quite a holiday feeling that the youngsters watched the team fade into the distance as they speculated on what wonders its load might contain when it again came over the hill in two or three days.

A couple of hours on the easy going of the firm, wind-packed snow of the ridges brought Bill and Jane to Rocky Cove where they stopped briefly for a cup of tea and a yarn with the first of their neighbors that they had not seen for two months. From

Rocky Cove the way lay mostly on the ice to Rigolet and their arrival there was before sundown. Putting up at the Hudson's Bay Company's kitchen, where open house was kept for travellers, they spent the evening visiting the few households of the tiny village and the next day settled to their trading. By the time this was finished it was too late to leave Rigolet and a second night was spent in the cheery company of friends who had not been seen for months and might not again be seen for many more. It was in the graying dawn of their third day from home that Bill lashed up his load and harnessed his team for the return trip.

When the red rim of the sun turned the sea ice to a crimson plain at the purple-shadowed feet of the hills they were five or six miles on their way. The day promised to be fair as the frosty vapor from the panting breaths of the dogs hung in the still air. They stopped again for a brief warm-up and a snack at Rocky Cove before starting the last 15 miles across the neck to home. It was with a slight feeling of unease that Bill noticed the beginning of a wispy cloud formation to the eastward as they pulled away from Rocky Cove and began the ascent to the ridges. The evening was calm and fine, however, and he reckoned that the two-hour run to home would be safely done long before any bad weather moved in.

The only worrisome thing was that his was a young team and the year-old pup he was training to be a leader seemed to have little sense. The old leader that had died last fall could have been trusted to take them home no matter how thick the weather, without deviating a whisker's length from the trail. Bill didn't quite know if he could trust the pup who always seemed to want to be told where to go. It was clouding in rapidly now and though still calm the very stillness held the menace of something waiting to pounce.

Halfway across the neck the first few snowflakes began to fall, and as darkness curtained the rocky slopes the first searching fingers of icy wind stirred the gathering powder into feathery swirls and dragged them, rustling, across the tops of the drifts. In the space of a quarter of an hour it was blowing a gale and in the black of the night the thickening snow blotted everything from sight in a weaving wall of wind and pelting icy particles. The team faltered, slowed and stopped. The young leader had no confidence in his ability to stay on the trail, and his mates shared his uncertainty. Unable to see more than a few yards, Bill began to consider the advisability of finding a hollow sheltered enough to burrow into the snow for the night. Though this would mean a risk of freezing, it might present a better chance of survival than would be offered by blundering blindly on with a very good chance of plunging over a cliff. Already the biting wind was beginning to leave little spots of frost bite on any exposed skin and it wouldn't be too long before Bill and Jane began to freeze quite badly.

Bill knew that they were still on the trail, for just there by his leader a pyramid-shaped cairn of rocks marked where the Big Brook trail came in from the north to join their own. He walked out through the team and stood by the cairn, recalling to mind the various folds in the nearby land that might offer shelter enough to permit them to get through this night. As he stood, the voice of another driver reached his ears, the voice of a man urging his team onward, and, as he looked, a team surged out of the swirling darkness. Nine black and white dogs trotted by almost near enough to touch. On the komatik behind them knelt a lone man who gestured urgently at Bill to follow before he turned again to face his team. Bill's own dogs, crazy with excitement, were already lunging into their traces and as the komatik slid by him he dropped to his seat on the load. Though the other team was a strange one to him the driver seemed to know where he was going, for he drove with the assurance of a man whose leader had been over the road before.

For an hour the two teams trotted steadily through the swirling blackness, Bill's young team straining against their heavy load to let the young leader keep his nose almost touching the stern of the leading komatik. On some of the steeper grades where the weight of their load threatened to cause them to fall behind, the black team slowed a little to let them keep up. Bill marvelled at the control the stranger had over his team, for he was travelling light and could easily run them out of sight in no time. It wasn't till a faint spark of light through the storm showed where the house lay ahead that the strange team drew ahead in a burst of speed.

Back at the house the youngsters had been having a grand time. Joe had had one day hunting ptarmigan on the ridges above the house. The second day he had harnessed up his own team of pups and gone out to the summer place, where a day on the ice foot by the open sea had yielded some of the big eider ducks that make a fine Christmas dinner. Both days, with her housework done, Janet had spent some hours fishing through the ice at the mouth of the brook, and several dozen trout and a few hundred smelt had been added to the stock of frozen fish in the bins of the storehouse. The third day they both stayed close to home, and from noon on many were the glances they took at the trail from the hills where their parents' team should appear any time now. The first twinges of anxiety began as the weather worsened at dusk. The coming of full darkness brought with it a wind that roared off the hills and drove icy scuds of drift rattling across the window panes. The youngsters were silently thoughtful as they sat down to supper. Both hoped that the storm had struck on the other side of the neck early enough to cause their parents to stay the night at Rocky Cove.

Supper was barely over when a chorus of welcoming yelps and howls from Joe's pups brought them to their feet to stare through the windows. A team, not their father's, but a team of nine big black and white dogs, drew up to the door and stopped at a low-voiced command from the driver. Joe hastily pulled on his jacket and cap to go out and welcome the stranger and Janet watched as the dogs, in the usual fashion of a team glad to have reached the end of a hard day, rolled and rubbed their faces in the snow to rid their eyes of the accumulation of frost from their breaths. The driver stood for a moment by his komatik and coiled up his long whip as he waited for some sign from within.

As Janet watched, Joe appeared from the lean-to porch and walked into the square of lamplight from the window. The leader, a huge, powerful-looking beast, gambolled playfully toward him and Joe stooped to pull its harness off. As he reached for the leader Joe stopped and gazed unbelieving at his hands, for there was nothing between them. There on the wind-swept deck he was alone, more alone than he had ever been in his life, for nine big dogs with their driver and the big tripping komatik had vanished. Joe turned and started back to the door, worried by what little Janet, watching from the window, might be making of this. As he reached for the latch-string an uproar of welcome again broke from his team of pups tethered in the edge of the woods. This time, as he turned to face whatever might be coming, it was his father's familiar team that trotted jauntily on to the lamp-lit deck.

The dogs crowded around Joe, rubbing their bodies against his legs, each frantic to draw his attention and be the next unharnessed. It wasn't till Joe had sorted out and coiled up the mass of sealskin traces that he approached the komatik to help his father unlash and carry in the load. As he straightened from his bent position to coil the long lash-line Bill asked, "What became of the team that came in ahead of us?"

Joe hoisted a heavy sack to his shoulder and turned toward the house. "There was no team," he answered quietly.

Conversations With the Little Table

Robertson Davies

Massey College is troubled with ghosts, much as lesser fabrics are troubled with mice; the most resolute determination is powerless to keep them away. Until this year, however, I have congratulated myself that they have kept clear of the part of the College that is reserved for the private quarters of myself and my family. Only once, many years ago, did a ghost tap at my bedroom door, and when I answered he quickly led me into the College proper. But of course a time had to come when I would find a ghost in the Lodgings. Anyone could have foreseen it.

It has always been my desire to keep my private life and my college life apart. If the ghost that visited me in the Master's Lodging had been a personal spectre, I would not trouble you about the matter now. But he had an undoubted relationship with the College as a whole; indeed it might be said that he was, at least in origin, a source of pride to the College. Two apparently unconnected happenings brought him here. The first was the publication, during the year past, of Colonel Stacey's book *A Very Double Life*, about some aspects of the personal character of the late William Lyon Mackenzie King;

it was a significant book, deservedly successful with the public, and I recall with what pleasure we toasted it, and its author, at High Table, where we always celebrate the achievements of members of our community. The other fact was that one of my daughters moved to Hamilton, and bought a house there.

How could two such unrelated happenings work together to produce a result in Massey College? Those of you who have had experience of the occult world know that there is no chance assembly of facts that may not rouse an echo in the world of spirits. It happened like this: another of my daughters, who lives in Ottawa, wanted to send her sister a gift for her new home; she brought it to Toronto and left it with my wife and myself to be collected by the Hamilton daughter at some convenient time. It was a charming gift, a small table of the kind that antique dealers call an 'occasional table', an antique of attested Canadian craftsmanship. It was as a piece of Canadiana that its quality as a gift was raised above the commonplace; in every other respect it was just a nice little table.

'Where did it come from?' I asked my daughter.

'Oh, it has what the antique dealer called provenance,' she replied; 'it came from the house of an Ottawa lady named Mrs. Patteson, who was quite well known in her time as a collector of unusual things, and unusual people.'

The name meant nothing to me. We put the table in a room in our basement, to wait until it was picked up. And for a number of reasons, that was not speedily.

This was in the early autumn, and until November the table remained where it had been put. It was on the night of November the first—All Souls' Eve, as you will immediately have recognized—that I heard an unusual sound just after I had gone to bed; unusual because it was faint, but persistent. Loud sounds are not unknown in this neighbourhood during the night. Sounds attaining to the state of uproar may be heard, as students from the neighbouring colleges and residences rage through the streets, uttering cries which mount to the level of the Primal Scream. But this sound suggested a low but persistent tapping, as though someone were knocking; not the kind of knocking that one associates with academic communities—the tireless knocking of reputations and institutions—but a light hammering. I strove to ignore it, but at last I rose and put on slippers and dressing-gown, and set out in search.

It was clear as soon as I left my bedroom that the sound was inside my own house, and my ear directed me to the cellar, to the door of a room not much used, where the Ottawa table was stored. I opened the door slowly, and to my astonishment the room was suffused with a soft light—a mauve light—strongest in an open space in which stood the Little Table, and—wondrous in the telling—the Little Table seemed to be dancing a jig.

Far be it from me to pretend that I am a man of unusual courage, but in my own house I suffer no nonsense from anything, animate or inanimate. I put my hand on the Table and forced it to stand still. But when I took my hand away something happened that shattered my self-possession: the table moved toward me and began to rub itself against me in a manner that suggested a dog, but a dog with a more than dog-like intelligence. The table was fondling me.

I am sure that many of you are acquainted with the book on Canadian furniture written by the great expert on that subject, Scott Symons; in it he asserts that Canadian furniture, at its finest, has a sensuous quality that can be, in certain instances, positively erotic. He says—and I have no reason to doubt his word—that on one occasion, during a meal, a dining table caressed his knee. Ghosts I can cope with, but erotic furniture destroys my self-possession; I rushed out of the room and upstairs, where my wife was still reading.

'You are pale,' said she; 'you look as if you had seen a ghost.'

'Not this time,' I replied; 'it's that table downstairs. It tried to get fresh with me. I think I need a drink.'

An ordinary woman might have laughed, or offered to get the drink, or perhaps some aspirin. But my wife is not an ordinary woman. She rose at once, tucked the book she was reading under her arm, and led the way back to the mysterious chamber.

The mauve light flickered eerily, and as we went in the table's movement—it was like dancing—became almost frantic. My wife drew two chairs up to it, one on each side, and nodded to me to sit down. Then, to my astonishment, she placed her hands on the top of the table, with the fingers spread wide, and again nodded to me to do the same, with the ends of my fingers touching hers.

The response of the table was extraordinary. If ever a table might be said to give a sigh of relief, that was what it did. It became quiet, and almost soft under our hands; it seemed to be waiting.

'What's up?' I whispered.

My wife said nothing, but nodded to her book, which she had placed on the floor. I saw that it was Colonel Stacey's book, *A Very Double Life*.

'This must be the Little Table,' she said.

It is a commonplace to say that women have extraordinary powers of intuition. As soon as she had spoken I understood the connection. Because, as those of you know who have read it, that book describes how the late Prime Minister, and his lifelong friend and associate in spiritualism, Mrs. Patteson, used to spend long, rapt hours with a Little Table, by means of which they communicated with the spirits of the dead. Little Table; Mrs. Patteson; at last I understood.

The Little Table! The table dignified, or perhaps I should say hallowed, by all those conversations Mr. King recorded in his diary, and Professor Stacey had made known to us. I felt myself uplifted, to be thus involved with—and indeed snuggled up to by—an object so rich in association. The psychic history of Canada is scant, and here I was, so to speak, getting in on the ground floor! I felt myself unworthy. I felt that I should at once telephone to Professor Stacey, or to Maurice Careless, and ask them to come at once for—well, for what? I didn't know what the Little Table had, so to speak, on its mind.

I know the proceeding for getting answers from tables when they are in a communicative mood. I spoke.

'The usual thing, I presume?' I said. 'One rap for yes; two for no, and otherwise raps in series indicating the letters of the alphabet. Is that what you have in mind?'

Firmly, and it seemed to me joyously, the Little Table

knocked once. That is to say it gave a quick tap with one tiny hoof upon the floor. It had said Yes.

'Are you there, Mrs. Patteson?' I said.

Two taps, in rather a pettish mood.

'Then who are you?' said I.

The table burst into a gunfire of tapping that startled me. 'Just a minute,' I said; 'not quite so fast.' Again the table rattled out its message. I am not at my best when confronted with problems involving figures. There seemed to be a great many taps. 'Did you say Z?' I asked. 'No, no,' my wife whispered; 'it was twenty-one taps. What is twenty-one? How many letters are there in the alphabet?' 'Twenty-eight, of course,' I hissed. 'Would you mind repeating?'

The Little Table gave two vicious little kicks, one to each side. My wife took it on the ankle, I on the shin. Then it rattled away in its telegraphic style, like one of those old-fashioned Morse instruments one heard clicking in the railway stations of an earlier day.

It was hopeless. 'Will you wait a moment,' said I. 'I want to make a helpful little chart.'

It used to be said that cobbler's children were always barefoot; by some kindred freak of Fate author's houses are always barren of pencils and paper. But at last I found what I wanted, and laboriously wrote out the alphabet, which – try as I might – proved to have only twenty-six letters, and to each letter I assigned a number. I didn't quite dare to lay this handy device on the Little Table; I feared it might scorn the simplicity of my mind. So I put it beside me on the floor. 'Now fire away,' I said; 'who is speaking, please?'

Spiteful little beast that it was, the table now tapped with tedious, insulting slowness. But at least it was possible to follow its message. Twenty-three taps.

'V,' said my wife. 'No, no; it was X,' said I.

Again those spiteful kicks. I should explain that the Little Table had what furniture experts call 'ball-and-claw feet,' and it hurt. Then it tapped again, even more slowly.

This time we got it right. 'W,' we exclaimed in concert. The table tapped once.

'A,' said I.

'No, it means yes,' said my wife. 'It was W.'

Next time, twelve slow taps. L. Then thirteen taps. M. Then eleven taps. K.

'W L M K,' said I. 'Doesn't mean a thing.'

I still bear the marks of the ferocious attack of the ball-and-claw feet. But I have mentioned that women have extraordinary intuition. 'William Lyon Mackenzie King,' said my wife, in a low, reverential tone; 'it must be Mr. King himself.'

We rose and bowed to the Little Table, and it tipped its stout little person in ceremonious acknowledgement.

When I am not on duty as Master of this College I allow myself to use certain slang expressions that were current in my youth. 'Now we're cooking with gas,' I said. And the Little Table rapped once. Yes.

What should I say? Once, in my youth, I met Mr. King. He was old and near to death: I was young and impressionable, and I still remember the penetration of his glance, which seemed to be looking right through me, and weighing my possible value to the Liberal Party. He did not speak. I said – I remember the phrase perfectly, because it seemed to me to be particularly apt, under the circumstances – I said, 'How do you do, Sir?' Now I said it again, taking up the conversation from the point where it had been dropped all those many years ago.

The Little Table tapped briskly, now. Nine: pause; one, thirteen: pause; twenty-two, five, eighteen, twenty-five; pause: twenty-three, five, twelve, and twelve again. 'He said, "I am very well," I whispered to my wife. 'I know,' said she: 'I was counting.'

I shall not give you all the detail of the conversation that followed. The counting was hard work, not merely because Mr. King was a somewhat impetuous rapper, but because he was, to my surprise, an impressionistic speller. So I shall merely tell you what was said, shorn of all the psychic trappings.

'Am I to infer that you are among the Blessed?' said I.

The answer, now I reflect on it, was ambiguous. 'I am among friends,' said WLMK.

'Liberals?' I asked.

'Naturally,' came the reply.

'Ask him about Sir Wilfrid Laurier,' my wife prompted.

'Is Sir Wilfrid with you?'

One rap. 'Yes.'

'Happy, I trust?'

Here the Little Table seemed to lose control of itself. It tapped very rapidly, in a singular rhythm; eight-one, eight-one, eight-one. Which, as you have immediately grasped, is Ha, Ha, Ha! Then some very rapid tapping which, so far as I could follow it, said something about somebody's nose being out of joint. Then the laughing signal again. I was about to ask if Sir Wilfrid had suffered some posthumous damage to his nose, and how, and why, but I saw my wife frowning and shaking her head. So I dropped the subject of Sir Wilfrid.

What next? Extraordinary as it may seem, I could not think of a thing to say to the spirit of Mr. King. My wife saw that I was at a loss. 'Try him about his dog,' said she.

'Dog?' said I, not understanding.

'Pat,' said she; 'his dear doggie, his greatest friend.'

I have never cared much for dogs. But I know that dog-lovers are susceptible to flattery on the subject of their pets, and I felt that I had put my foot in it about Sir Wilfrid Laurier, and must recover lost ground. 'How's Pat?' I asked.

The table seemed to brighten up. It did some frisky tapping. Two-fifteen-twenty-three: twenty-three-fifteen-twenty-three. Bow-wow. Obviously it was Pat himself talking, so I feigned great benevolence and patted the table with the *faux bonhomie* I adopt toward other people's dogs. The table responded by rapping twenty-three, fifteen, fifteen again, and six. Woof. And, so far as I was concerned, that was enough from Pat.

I thought of people in the Other World from whom I might like to have a message. Vincent Massey, of course! Often, since his death, I have wished I could have the benefit of his advice. 'How is Mr. Massey?' I asked. The table tapped sulkily for a few seconds.

'Don't know and don't care,' was the message.

I remembered what I should have thought of earlier. Mr. King and Mr. Massey had not seen eye to eye.

'Still scrapping,' I whispered to my wife. But the Little Table overheard me, and tapped some very rapid comment which caught me off my guard, so that I was only able to transcribe the words 'opinionated,' 'insubordinate' and 'elitist'. But whether they referred to Mr. Massey or to me, I cannot say.

This was discouraging. I saw no reason why I should sit in this College and listen to Mr. King being nasty about its Founder. But what was there to say? He seemed to be so touchy. Then I had what I supposed was a happy inspiration. I noticed the copy of *A Very Double Life* that my wife had placed on the floor beside her.

'Have you read Colonel Stacey's book?' I asked.

There was a significant pause. Then a single rap. Yes,

'It's selling very well,' I said, glad to be on an ample and chatty theme at last. 'You must be pleased.'

It seemed to me that the temperature in the room dropped suddenly. 'Oh, you think that, do you?' rapped the Little Table, with unusual deliberation. I was overcome by one of my terrible failures of tact. I am generally pretty good at tact, but as it is an acquired faculty with me, and not an inherent trait, I sometimes put my foot in it, when talking to difficult people. 'I suppose you are glad to be an object of so much interest,' I said.

The Little Table rapped and rapped and rapped. 'I should have thought that my career offered enough of interest to the people of the country to which I devoted the whole of my career *comma* and my not inconsiderable talents,' it said, 'without a discussion of my youthful work among fallen women. Poor *comma* unhappy creatures *dash* 'soiled doves' was the term I always applied to them when I thought about them *dash* I went among them with but one thought in mind. I sought *comma* by talking to them seriously and sympathetically about the principles of Liberalism *comma* to win them from a life of shame to useful political activity. But so far as I could discover, not one of them ever went to the polls to cast the vote which was her democratic birth-right. I should have thought that in the present enthusiasm for Women's Liberation *dash* a cause very dear to my heart, as it was near to the heart of the noble woman who was the inspiration of all that was best in me *dash* I allude, needless to say, to my dear Mother–' And here there was a pause, which, as an old *aficionado* of political meetings I knew was meant for applause, so I applauded loudly; after I had made my hands very red, the Little Table resumed. 'I should have thought, I say, that my name would be mentioned as one of the earliest enthusiasts for the Women's Cause *semi-colon* that I should be mentioned with Henrik Ibsen *comma* with Bernard Shaw *comma* with the sainted Christabel Pankhurst and the never sufficiently to be lauded Nellie McClung. But it was not to be. No *comma* it has been suggested that my interest in women was of a carnal origin. And all because Jack Pickersgill hadn't the common gumption to destroy those damned diaries. Now you listen to me, young man–' and the Little Table rapped on and on. I was so stunned to be addressed as 'young man' that I forgot to count, and I observed that my wife was becoming drowsy under the spell of Mr. King's platform style and the tediousness of all that rapped-out punctuation. At last, after something like half an hour of telegraphed eloquence, the Little Table was still.

'Sorry about that,' said I. 'But I'm afraid there's nothing I can do about it. Shall I arrange an encounter with the author of the book? Would you like to rap with Colonel Stacey?'

Two decisive raps. No. And that was all. Worn out with our night listening to the mighty dead, my wife and I crept upstairs, to seek much needed repose.

I wanted to go back the next night, but my wife disagreed. 'He'll make another speech,' said she. 'Besides, I think it's unlucky to quarrel with spirits. Leave the wretched table alone, and I'll get it out of the house as soon as I can.' And there, for some time, the matter rested.

There is in my nature a generous portion of curiosity. I make no apology for it, and indeed I encourage and cherish it. Curiosity is part of the cement that holds society together; for many years I was a journalist, and a journalist without curiosity is useless. After Quebec's historic decision in the election of November 15 you will understand how I itched to have another talk with the Little Table. There must be something to be got out of the ghost of Mackenzie King, some scoop which I could, at the right moment, reveal to the world. So, after a few weeks of iron self-control, I broke down, and crept away by myself to the room in the depths of my house.

It was December the sixth when I went to the room where the Little Table was. My spirits rose as I saw that the glow of purple light arose from it, even more intense than it had been before. Would I be able to establish contact through it, I wondered, without the help of another person? I sat down and placed my hands, fingers spread, on its surface. I need not have worried; immediately I felt the thrill that told me the Little Table was ready to speak.

'Mr. King, are you there?' I whispered.

The retort was not in the best of humour. 'What do you think?' the table rapped. 'You've been away long enough. What brings you here now?'

'It is the sixth of December,' I said.

'What of it?' rapped the table.

'It is St. Nicholas's day,' I replied. 'He has always been kind to me.'

'Do you expect me as a Presbyterian, to pay attention to such rubbish,' said the spirit of Mackenzie King, in a series of short, brittle raps.

Off to a bad start, I thought. It is one of my weaknesses to imagine that everybody shares my enthusiasm for saints. The Little Table was clicking on.

'Superstition will be the ruin of you, Davies,' it said. 'I have seen many a man of minor talents, like yourself, go utterly to pot because of superstition. Brace up, man, *comma* brace up.'

Look who's talking, I thought. This is the man who spent so many of his private hours talking to spirits by means of this very Little Table at which I now sit. This is the man who addresses me by this tedious, farcical business of table-rapping, instead of manifesting himself and talking to me ghost to man, as a serious spirit should. But I subdued my indignation and spoke gently.

'I have come,' I said, 'because I hope that you will favour me with an exclusive interview. I should greatly value your opinion of the present state of Confederation. Taking the long view—which I assume is one of the prerogatives of your present position—what do you think is likely to happen in Quebec? Is Separatism a political gambit or a genuine threat?'

There was a pause. Then—'Don't trouble me with such nonsense,' rapped Mr. King. 'Do you suppose I have nothing to keep me busy here? My present Cabinet demands the most careful management, in spite of my success in bringing about a decisive Tory overthrow—'

I could hold in no longer. For the first time, I interrupted the Little Table. I seized it and held it firmly to the ground, thereby, so to speak, choking Mr. King off in mid-speech. This was precisely what I wanted.

'Cabinet?' I said. 'Tory overthrow? Do you mean that you are in power in—in—?' I did not know how to finish the question.

'The greatest victory of my career,' came the reply. 'I have reduced the Tories to a miserable, seedy rump, and their Leader is trying to prevent a final break.'

'What Leader?' said I, breathless with curiosity.

'Who has always been the leader of the Conservative Party, whatever puppet may have appeared to mortal eyes to hold that office?' said Mr. King.

I knew, of course. That is to say, I knew who had always appeared to Mr. King to be the Tory Leader. My mind trembled on the verge of total disorder. 'Mr. King,' I whispered, 'are you telling me that you have brought about Separatism in—' But I did not like to speak the word. To a Presbyterian it might seem offensive. I changed the form of the question. 'Mr. King,' said I; 'where are you?'

At that instant, it seemed to me that the Little Table became extremely hot. But it tapped merrily. And what it tapped amazed me greatly. Mr. King was not a slangy man, but I suppose that when he was a youth, an undergraduate in this University, he had acquired a few of the slang expressions of his contemporaries. Anyhow, what the Little Table rapped, almost giggling as it did so, was: 'None of your beeswax!'

'But Mr. King!' I persisted. 'Don't leave me just yet. You must know that your successor on earth has recently been described in an extremely influential American newspaper as "perhaps the world's most gifted leader". Tell me something helpful that I may pass on to Pierre Elliot Trudeau.'

The table stopped its giggling in an instant. It became, not hot, but icy cold. 'You tell Trudeau this from me!' it banged – yes, it banged on the floor. And then it began to tap so fast that it took all my concentration to make out the letters of its clumsy, rattling language. They seemed to mean little, until I understood that the tapping was now in French. But what French! It was politician's French, which is a language in itself, understood by few. I could not make out, with clarity, what Mr. King wanted me to tell Mr. Trudeau, except that he seemed to be summoning him to join himself, wherever he was, with the utmost speed. Mr. King seemed to have a place for Mr. Trudeau in his new dominion, but I gathered that it was not in the Cabinet. I thought I caught something about 'the hot-seat.'

The Little Table was not made to withstand such vehemence. At the height of the tirade, one of the little feet broke off, and suddenly there was silence.

I had the Little Table mended, the next day, by Norbert. He said he had a suitable piece of wood, which he had taken out of one of the fixtures of the College Chapel, that would do the job almost invisibly.

But the Little Table never spoke again. I suppose there are things, such as pieces of wood from our Chapel, that are intolerable to Presbyterian ghosts, and especially those who have achieved Separatism by what used to be called the Harrowing of Hell.

Shoeless Joe Jackson Comes to Iowa

W. P. Kinsella

My father said he saw him years later playing in a tenth-rate commercial league in a textile town in Carolina, wearing shoes and an assumed name.

"He'd put on 50 pounds and the spring was gone from his step in the outfield, but he could still hit. Oh, how that man could hit. No-one has ever been able to hit like Shoeless Joe."

Two years ago at dusk on a spring evening, when the sky was a robin's-egg blue and the wind as soft as a day-old chick, as I was sitting on the verandah of my farm home in eastern Iowa, a voice very clearly said to me, "If you build it, he will come."

The voice was that of a ballpark announcer. As he spoke, I instantly envisioned the finished product I knew I was being asked to conceive. I could see the dark, squarish speakers, like ancient sailors' hats, attached to aluminum-painted light standards that glowed down into a baseball field, my present position being directly behind home plate.

In reality, all anyone else could see out there in front of me was a tattered lawn of mostly dandelions and quack grass that petered out at the edge of a cornfield perhaps 50 yards from the house.

Anyone else was my wife Annie, my daughter Karin, a corn-coloured collie named Carmeletia Pope, and a cinnamon and white guinea pig named Junior who ate spaghetti and sang each time the fridge door opened. Karin and the dog were not quite two years old.

"If you build it, he will come," the announcer repeated in scratchy Middle American, as if his voice had been recorded on an old 78-rpm record.

A three-hour lecture or a 500-page guide book could not have given me clearer directions: dimensions of ballparks jumped over and around me like fleas, cost figures for light standards and floodlights whirled around my head like the moths that dusted against the porch light above me.

That was all the instruction I ever received: two announcements and a vision of a baseball field. I sat on the verandah until the satiny dark was complete. A few curdly clouds striped the moon and it became so silent I could hear my eyes blink.

Our house is one of those massive old farm homes, square as a biscuit box with a sagging verandah on three sides. The floor of the verandah slopes so that marbles, baseballs, tennis balls and ball bearings all accumulate in a corner like a herd of cattle clustered with their backs to a storm. On the north verandah is a wooden porch swing where Annie and I sit on humid August nights, sip lemonade from teary glasses, and dream.

When I finally went to bed, and after Annie inched into my arms in that way she has, like a cat that you suddenly find sound asleep in your lap, I told her about the voice and I told her that I knew what it wanted me to do.

"Oh love," she said, "if it makes you happy you should do it," and she found my lips with hers, and I shivered involuntarily as her tongue touched mine.

Annie: she has never once called me crazy. Just before I started the first landscape work, as I stood looking out at the lawn and the cornfield wondering how it could look so different in daylight, considering the notion of accepting it all as a dream and abandoning it, Annie appeared at my side and her arm circled my waist. She leaned against me and looked up, cocking her head like one of the red squirrels that scamper along the power lines from the highway to the house. "Do it, love," she said, as I looked down at her, that slip of a girl with hair the colour of cayenne pepper and at least a million freckles on her face and arms, that girl who lives in blue jeans and T-shirts and at 24 could still pass for sixteen.

I thought back to when I first knew her. I came to Iowa to study. She was the child of my landlady. I heard her one afternoon outside my window as she told her girlfriends, "When I grow up I'm going to marry . . ." and she named me. The others were going to be nurses, teachers, pilots or movie stars, but Annie chose me as her occupation. She was ten. Eight years later we were married. I chose willingly, lovingly to stay in Iowa, eventually rented this farm, bought this farm, operating it one inch from bankruptcy. I don't seem meant to farm, but I want to be close to this precious land, for Annie and me to be able to say, "This is ours."

Now I stand ready to cut into the cornfield, to chisel away a piece of our livelihood to use as dream currency, and Annie says, "Oh, love, if it makes you happy you should do it." I carry her words in the back of my mind, stored the way a maiden aunt might wrap a brooch, a remembrance of a long-lost love. I understand how hard that was for her to say and how it got harder as the project advanced. How she must have told her family not to ask me about the baseball field I was building, because they stared at me dumb-eyed, a row of silent, thickset peasants with red faces. Not an imagination among them except to forecast the wrath of God that will fall on the heads of pagans such as I.

He, of course, was Shoeless Joe Jackson.

Joseph Jefferson (Shoeless Joe) Jackson
Born: Brandon Mills, S.C., 16 July, 1887
Died: Greenville, S.C., 5 December, 1951

In April, 1945, Ty Cobb picked Shoeless Joe as the best left fielder of all time.

He never learned to read or write. He created legends with

a bat and a glove. He wrote records with base hits, his pen a bat, his book History.

Was it really a voice I heard? Or was it perhaps something inside me making a statement that I did not hear with my ears but with my heart? Why should I want to follow this command? But as I ask, I already know the answer. I count the loves in my life: Annie, Karin, Iowa, Baseball. The great god Baseball.

My birthstone is a diamond. When asked, I say my astrological sign is "hit and run," which draws a lot of blank stares here in Iowa where 30,000 people go to see the University of Iowa Hawkeyes football team while 30 regulars, including me, watch the baseball team perform.

My father, I've been told, talked baseball statistics to my mother's belly while waiting for me to be born.

My father: born, Glen Ullin, N.D., 14 April, 1896. Another diamond birthstone. Never saw a professional baseball game until 1919 when he came back from World War I where he was gassed at Passchendaele. He settled in Chicago where he inhabited a room above a bar across from Comiskey Park and quickly learned to live and die with the White Sox. Died a little when, as prohibitive favourites, they lost the 1919 World Series to Cincinnati, died a lot the next summer when eight members of the team were accused of throwing that World Series.

Before I knew what baseball was, I knew of Connie Mack, John McGraw, Grover Cleveland Alexander, Ty Cobb, Babe Ruth, Tris Speaker, Tinker-to-Evers-to-Chance, and, of course, Shoeless Joe Jackson. My father loved underdogs, cheered for the Brooklyn Dodgers and the hapless St. Louis Browns, loathed the Yankees, which I believe was an inherited trait, and insisted that Shoeless Joe was innocent, a victim of big business and crooked gamblers.

That first night, immediately after the voice and the vision, I did nothing except sip my lemonade a little faster and rattle the ice cubes in my glass. The vision of the baseball park lingered—swimming, swaying—seeming to be made of red steam, though perhaps it was only the sunset. There was a vision within the vision: one of Shoeless Joe Jackson playing left field. Shoeless Joe Jackson who last played major league baseball in 1920 and was suspended for life, along with seven of his compatriots, by Commissioner Keneshaw Mountain Landis, for his part in throwing the 1919 World Series.

"He hit .375 against the Reds in the 1919 World Series and played errorless ball," my father would say, scratching his head in wonder.

Instead of nursery rhymes, I was raised on the story of the Black Sox Scandal, and instead of Tom Thumb or Rumpelstiltskin, I grew up hearing of the eight disgraced ballplayers: Weaver, Cicotte, Risberg, Felsch, Gandil, Williams, McMullin, and always, Shoeless Joe Jackson.

"Twelve hits in an eight-game series. And *they* suspended *him,*" father would cry, and Shoeless Joe became a symbol of the tyranny of the powerful over the powerless. The name Keneshaw Mountain Landis became synonymous with the Devil.

It is more work than you might imagine to build a baseball field. I laid out a whole field, but it was there in spirit only. It was really only left field that concerned me. Home plate was made from pieces of cracked two-by-four imbedded in the earth. The pitcher's mound rocked like a cradle when I stood on it. The bases were stray blocks of wood, unanchored. There was no backstop or grandstand, only one shaky bleacher beyond the left field wall. There was a left field wall, but only about 50 feet of it, twelve feet high, stained dark green and braced from the rear. And the left field grass. My intuition told me that it was the grass that was important. It took me three seasons to hone that grass to its proper texture, to its proper colour. I made trips to Minneapolis and one or two other cities where the stadiums still have natural grass infields and outfields. I would arrive hours before a game and watch the groundskeepers groom the field like a prize animal, then stay after the game when in the cool of the night the same groundsmen appeared with hoses, hoes, rakes, and patched the grasses like medics attending wounded soldiers.

I pretended to be building a little league ballfield and asked their secrets and sometimes was told. I took interest in their total operation; they wouldn't understand if I told them I was building only a left field.

Three seasons I've spent seeding, watering, fussing, praying, coddling that field like a sick child until it glows parrot-green, cool as mint, soft as moss, lying there like a cashmere blanket. I began watching it in the evenings, sitting on the rickety bleacher just beyond the fence. A bleacher I had constructed for an audience of one.

My father played some baseball, Class B teams in Florida and California. I found his statistics in a dusty minor league record book. In Florida, he played for a team called the Angels and, by his records, was a better-than-average catcher. He claimed to have visited all 48 states and every major-league ballpark before, at 40, he married and settled down a two-day drive from the nearest major league team. I tried to play, but ground balls bounced off my chest and fly balls dropped between my hands. I might have been a fair designated hitter, but the rule was too late in coming.

There is the story of the urchin who, tugging at Shoeless Joe Jackson's sleeve as he emerged from a Chicago courthouse, said, "Say it ain't so, Joe."

Jackson's reply reportedly was, "I'm afraid it is, kid."

When he comes, I won't put him on the spot by asking. The less said the better. It is likely that he did accept some money from gamblers. But throw the Series? Never! Shoeless Joe led both teams in hitting in that 1919 Series. It was the circumstances. The circumstances. The players were paid peasant salaries while the owners became rich. The infamous Ten Day Clause, which voided contracts, could end any player's career without compensation, pension, or even a ticket home.

The second spring, on a tooth-achy May evening, a covering of black clouds lumbered off westward like ghosts of buffalo and the sky became the cold colour of a silver coin. The forecast was for frost.

The left-field grass was like green angora, soft as a baby's cheek. In my mind I could see it dull and crisp, bleached by frost, and my chest tightened.

Then I used a trick a groundskeeper in Minneapolis taught

me, saying it was taught to him by grape farmers in California. I carried out a hose and making the spray so fine it was scarcely more than fog, I sprayed the soft, shaggy, spring grass all that chilled night. My hands ached and my own face became wet and cold, but as I watched, the spray froze on the grass, enclosing each blade in a gossamer-crystal coating of ice. A covering that served like a coat of armour to dispel the real frost that was set like a weasel upon killing in the night. I seemed to stand taller than ever before as the sun rose, turning the ice to eye-dazzling droplets, each a prism, making the field an orgy of rainbows.

Annie and Karin were at breakfast when I came in, the bacon and coffee smells and their laughter pulling me like a magnet.

"Did it work, love?" Annie asked, and I knew she knew by the look on my face that it did. And Karin, clapping her hands and complaining of how cold my face was when she kissed me, loved every second of it.

"And how did he get a name like Shoeless Joe?" I would ask my father, knowing full well the story but wanting to hear it again. And no matter how many times I heard it, I would still picture a lithe ballplayer, his great bare feet, white as baseballs, sinking into the outfield grass as he sprinted for a line drive. Then, after the catch, his toes gripping the grass like claws, he would brace and throw to the infield.

"It wasn't the least bit romantic," my dad would say. "When he was still in the minor leagues he bought a new pair of spikes and they hurt his feet; about the sixth inning he took them off and played the outfield in just his socks. The other players kidded him, called him Shoeless Joe, and the name stuck for all time."

It was hard for me to imagine that a sore-footed young outfielder taking off his shoes one afternoon not long after the turn of the century could generate a legend.

I came to Iowa to study, one of the thousands of faceless students who pass through large universities, but I fell in love with Iowa. Fell in love with the land, the people, with the sky, the cornfields and Annie. Couldn't find work in my field, took what I could get. For years, each morning I bathed and frosted my cheeks with Aqua Velva, donned a three-piece suit and snap-brim hat, and, feeling like Superman emerging from a telephone booth, set forth to save the world from a lack of life insurance. I loathed the job so much that I did it quickly, urgently, almost violently. It was Annie who got me to rent the farm. It was Annie who got me to buy it. I operate it the way a child fits together his first puzzle, awkwardly, slowly, but when a piece slips into the proper slot, with pride and relief and joy.

I built the field and waited, and waited, and waited.

"It will happen, honey," Annie would say when I stood shaking my head at my folly. People look at me. I must have a nickname in town. But I could feel the magic building like a storm gathering. It felt as if small animals were scurrying through my veins. I knew it was going to happen soon.

"There's someone on your lawn," Annie says to me, staring out into the orange-tinted dusk. "I can't see him clearly, but I can tell someone is there." She was quite right, at least about it being *my* lawn, although, it is not in the strictest sense of the word a lawn, it is a left field.

I watch Annie looking out. She is soft as a butterfly, Annie is, with an evil grin and a tongue that travels at the speed of light. Her jeans are painted to her body and her pointy little nipples poke at the front of a black T-shirt with the single word RAH! emblazoned in waspish yellow capitals. Her red hair is short and curly. She has the green eyes of a cat.

Annie understands, though it is me she understands, and not always what is happening. She attends ballgames with me and squeezes my arm when there's a hit, but her heart isn't in it and she would just as soon be at home. She loses interest if the score isn't close or the weather warm, or the pace fast enough. To me it is baseball and that is all that matters. It is the game that is important – the tension, the strategy, the ballet of the fielders, the angle of the bat.

I have been more restless than usual this night. I have sensed the magic drawing closer, hovering somewhere out in the night like a zeppelin, silky and silent, floating like the moon until the time is right.

Annie peeks through the drapes. "There *is* a man out there; I can see his silhouette. He's wearing a baseball uniform, an old-fashioned one."

"It's Shoeless Joe Jackson," I say. My heart sounds like someone flicking a balloon with their index finger.

"Oh," she says. Annie stays very calm in emergencies. She Band-aids bleeding fingers and toes, and patches the plumbing with gum and good wishes. Staying calm makes her able to live with me. The French have the right words for Annie – she has a good heart.

"Is he the Jackson on TV? The one you yell, 'Drop it, Jackson,' at?"

Annie's sense of baseball history is not highly developed.

"No, that's Reggie. This is Shoeless Joe Jackson. He hasn't played major league baseball since 1920."

"Well, aren't you going to go out and chase him off your lawn, or something?"

Yes. What am I going to do? I wish someone else understood. My daughter has an evil grin and bewitching eyes. She climbs into my lap and watches television baseball with me. There is a magic about her.

"I think I'll go upstairs and read for a while," Annie says. "Why don't you invite Shoeless Jack in for coffee?" I feel the greatest tenderness toward her then, something akin to the rush of love I felt the first time I held my daughter in my arms. Annie senses that magic is about to happen. She knows that she is not part of it. My impulse is to pull her to me as she walks by, the denim of her thighs making a tiny music. But I don't. She will be waiting for me and she will twine her body about me and find my mouth with hers.

As I step out on the verandah, I can hear the steady drone of the crowd, like bees humming on a white afternoon, and the voices of the vendors, like crows cawing.

A little ground mist, like wisps of gauze, snakes in slow circular motions just above the grass.

"The grass is soft as a child's breath," I say to the moonlight. On the porch wall I find the switch, and the single battery of floodlights I have erected behind the left-field fence sputters to life. "I've shaved it like a golf green, tended it like I would my own baby. It has been powdered and lotioned and loved. It is ready."

Moonlight butters the whole Iowa night. Clover and corn smells are thick as syrup. I experience a tingling like the tiniest of electric wires touching the back of my neck, sending warm sensations through me like the feeling of love. Then, as the lights flare, a scar against the blue-black sky, I see Shoeless Joe Jackson standing out in left field. His feet spread wide, body bent forward from the waist, hands on hips, he waits. There is the sharp crack of the bat and Shoeless Joe drifts effortlessly a few steps to his left, raises his right hand to signal for the ball, camps under it for a second or two, catches the ball, at the same time transferring it to his throwing hand, and fires it into the infield.

I make my way to the left field, walking in the darkness far outside the third-base line, behind where the third-base stands would be. I climb up on the wobbly bleacher behind the fence. I can look right down on Shoeless Joe. He fields a single on one hop and pegs the ball to third.

"How does it play?" I holler down.

"The ball bounces true," he replies.

"I know." I am smiling with pride and my heart thumps mightily against my ribs. "I've hit a thousand line drives and as many grounders. It's true as a felt-top table."

"It is," says Shoeless Joe. "It is true."

I lean back and watch the game. From where I sit the scene is as complete as in any of the major league baseball parks I have ever attended: the two teams, the stands, the fans, the lights, the vendors, the scoreboard. The only difference is that I sit alone in the left field bleacher and the only player who seems to have substance is Shoeless Joe Jackson. When Joe's team is at bat, the left fielder below me is transparent as if he were made of vapour. He performs mechanically, but seems not to have facial features. We do not converse.

A great amphitheatre of grandstand looms dark against the sky, the park is surrounded by decks of floodlights making it brighter than day, the crowd buzzes, the vendors hawk their wares, and I cannot keep the promise I made myself not to ask Shoeless Joe Jackson about his suspension and what it means to him.

While the pitcher warms up for the third inning we talk.

"It must have been . . . It must have been like . . ." but I can't find the words.

"Like having a part of me amputated, slick and smooth and painless, like having an arm or a leg taken off with one swipe of a scalpel, big and blue as a sword," and Joe looks up at me and his dark eyes seem about to burst with the pain of it. "A friend of mine used to tell about the war, how him and a buddy was running across a field when a piece of shrapnel took his friend's head off, and how the friend ran, headless, for several strides before he fell. I'm told that old men wake in the night and scratch itchy legs that have been dust for fifty years. That was me. Years and years later, I'd wake in the night with the smell of the ballpark in my nostrils and the cool of the grass on my feet. The thrill of the grass . . ."

How I wish my father could be here with me. He died before we had television in our part of the country. The very next year he could have watched in grainy black and white as Don Larsen pitched a no-hitter in the World Series. He would have loved hating the Yankees as they won that game. We were always going to go to a major-league baseball game, he and I. But the time was never right, the money always needed for something else. One of the last days of his life, late in the night while I sat with him because the pain wouldn't let him sleep, the radio dragged in a staticky station broadcasting a White Sox game. We hunched over the radio and cheered them on, but they lost. Dad told the story of the Black Sox Scandal for the last time. Told of seeing two of those World Series games, told of the way Shoeless Joe Jackson hit, told the dimensions of Comiskey Park, and how during the series the mobsters in striped suits sat in the box seats with their colourful women, watching the game and perhaps making plans to go out later and kill a rival.

"You must go," he said. "I've been in all sixteen major league parks. I want you to do it too. The summers belong to somebody else now, have for a long time." I nodded agreement.

"Hell, you know what I mean," he said, shaking his head. I did indeed.

"I loved the game," Shoeless Joe went on. "I'd have played for food money. I'd have played free and worked for food. It was the game, the parks, the smells, the sounds. Have you ever held a bat or a baseball to your face? The varnish, the leather. And it was the crowd, the excitement of them rising as one when the ball was hit deep. The sound was like a chorus. Then there was the chug-a-lug of the tin lizzies in the parking lots and the hotels with their brass spittoons in the lobbies and brass beds in the rooms. It makes me tingle all over like a kid on his way to his first double-header, just to talk about it."

The year after Annie and I were married, the year we first rented this farm, I dug Annie's garden for her; dug it by hand, stepping a spade into the soft black soil, ruining my salesman's hands. After I finished it rained, an Iowa spring rain as soft as spray from a warm hose. The clods of earth I had dug seemed to melt until the garden leveled out, looking like a patch of black ocean. It was near noon on a gentle Sunday when I walked out to that garden. The soil was soft and my shoes disappeared as I plodded until I was near the centre. There I knelt, the soil cool on my knees. I looked up at the low grey sky; the rain had stopped and the only sound was the surrounding trees dripping fragrantly. Suddenly I thrust my hands wrist-deep into the snuffy-black earth. The air was pure. All around me the clean smell of earth and water. Keeping my hands buried I stirred the earth with my fingers and I knew I loved Iowa as much as a man could love a piece of earth.

When I came back to the house Annie stopped me at the door, made me wait on the verandah, then hosed me down as if I were a door with too many handprints on it, while I tried to explain my epiphany. It is very difficult to describe an experience of religious significance while you are being sprayed with a garden hose by a laughing, loving woman.

"What happened to the sun?" Shoeless Joe says to me, waving his hand toward the banks of floodlights that surround the park.

"Only stadium in the big leagues that doesn't have them is

Wrigley Field," I say. "The owners found that more people could attend night games. They even play the World Series at night now."

Joe purses his lips, considering.

"It's harder to see the ball, especially at the plate."

"When there are breaks they usually go against the ballplayers, right? But I notice you're three for three so far," I add, looking down at his uniform, the only identifying marks a large S with an O in the top crook, an X in the bottom, and an American flag with 48 stars on his left sleeve near the elbow.

Joe grins. "I'd play for the Devil's own team just for the touch of a baseball. Hell, I'd play in the dark if I had to."

I want to ask about the day in December, 1951. If he'd lasted another few years things might have been different. There was a move afoot to have his record cleared, but it died with him. I wanted to ask, but my instinct told me not to. There are things it is better not to know.

It is one of those nights when the sky is close enough to touch, so close that looking up is like seeing my own eyes reflected in a rain barrel. I sit in the bleacher just outside the left field fence. I clutch in my hand a hot dog with mustard, onions and green relish. The voice of the crowd roars in my ears like the sea. Chords of the "Star-spangled Banner" and "Take Me Out to the Ballgame" float across the field. A Coke bottle is propped against my thigh, squat, greenish, the ice-cream-haired elf grinning conspiratorially from the cap.

Below me in left field, Shoeless Joe Jackson glides over the plush velvet grass, silent as a jungle cat. He prowls and paces, crouches ready to spring as, nearly 300 feet away, the ball is pitched. At the sound of the bat he wafts in whatever direction is required as if he were on ball bearings.

Then the intrusive sound of a screen door slamming reaches me, and I blink and start. I recognize it as the sound of the door to my house and looking into the distance, I can see a shape that I know is my daughter toddling down the back steps. Perhaps the lights or the crowd has awakened her and she has somehow eluded Annie. I judge the distance to the steps. I am just to the inside of the foul pole which is exactly 330 feet from home plate. I tense. Karin will surely be drawn to the lights and the emerald dazzle of the infield. If she touches anything, I fear it will all disappear, perhaps forever. Then as if she senses my discomfort she stumbles away from the lights, walking in the ragged fringe of darkness well outside the third-base line. She trails a blanket behind her, one tiny fist rubbing a sleepy eye. She is barefoot and wears a white flannelette nightgown covered in an explosion of daisies.

She climbs up the bleacher, alternating a knee and a foot on each step, and crawls into my lap, silently, like a kitten. I hold her close and wrap the blanket around her feet. The play goes on; her innocence has not disturbed the balance.

"What is it?" she says shyly, her eyes indicating that she means all that she sees.

"Just watch the left fielder," I say. "He'll tell you all you ever need to know about a baseball game. Watch his feet as the pitcher accepts the sign and gets ready to pitch. A good left fielder knows what pitch is coming and he can tell from the angle of the bat where the ball is going to be hit and, if he's good, how hard."

I look down at Karin. She cocks one sky-blue eye at me, wrinkling her nose, then snuggles into my chest the index finger of her right hand tracing tiny circles around her nose.

The crack of the bat is sharp as the yelp of a kicked cur. Shoeless Joe whirls, takes five loping strides directly toward us, turns again, reaches up, and the ball smacks into his glove. The final batter dawdles in the on-deck circle.

"Can I come back again?" Joe asks.

"I built this left field for you. It's yours any time you want to use it. They play 162 games a season now."

"There are others," he says. "If you were to finish the infield, why, old Chick Gandil could play first base, and we'd have the Swede at shortstop and Buck Weaver at third." I can feel his excitement rising. "We could stick McMullin in at second, and Cicotte and Lefty Williams would like to pitch again. Do you think you could finish the centre field? It would mean a lot to Happy Felsch."

"Consider it done," I say, hardly thinking of the time, the

money, the backbreaking labour it entails. "Consider it done," I say again, then stop suddenly as an idea creeps into my brain like a runner inching off first base.

"I know a catcher," I say. "He never made the majors, but in his prime he was good. Really good. Played Class B ball in Florida and California . . ."

"We could give him a try," says Shoeless Joe. "You give us a place to play and we'll look at your catcher."

I swear the stars have moved in close enough to eavesdrop as I sit in this single rickety bleacher that I built with my unskilled hands, looking down at Shoeless Joe Jackson. A breath of clover travels on the summer wind. Behind me, just yards away, brook water splashes softly in the darkness, a frog shrills, fireflies dazzle the night like red pepper. A petal falls.

"God, what an outfield," he says. "What a left field." He looks up at me and I look down at him. "This must be heaven," he says.

"No. It's Iowa," I reply automatically. But then I feel the night rubbing softly against my face like cherry blossoms; look at the sleeping girl-child in my arms, her small hand curled around one of my fingers; think of the fierce warmth of the woman waiting for me in the house; inhale the fresh-cut grass smell that seems locked in the air like permanent incense, and listen to the drone of the crowd, as below me Shoeless Joe Jackson tenses, watching the angle of the distant bat for a clue as to where the ball will be hit.

"I think you're right, Joe," I say, but softly enough not to disturb his concentration.

Buggam Grange: A Good Old Ghost Story

Stephen Leacock

The evening was already falling as the vehicle in which I was contained entered upon the long and gloomy avenue that leads to Buggam Grange.

A resounding shriek echoed through the wood as I entered the avenue. I paid no attention to it at the moment, judging it to be merely one of those resounding shrieks which one might expect to hear in such a place at such a time. As my drive continued, however, I found myself wondering in spite of myself why such a shriek should have been uttered at the very moment of my approach.

I am not by temperament in any degree a nervous man, and yet there was much in my surroundings to justify a certain feeling of apprehension. The Grange is situated in the loneliest part of England, the marsh country of the fens to which civilization has still hardly penetrated. The inhabitants, of whom there are only one and a half to the square mile, live here and there among the fens and eke out a miserable existence by frog fishing and catching flies. They speak a dialect so broken as to be practically unintelligible, while the perpetual rain which falls upon them renders speech itself almost superfluous.

Here and there where the ground rises slightly above the level of the fens there are dense woods tangled with parasitic creepers and filled with owls. Bats fly from wood to wood. The air on the lower ground is charged with the poisonous gases which exude from the marsh, while in the woods it is heavy with the dank odors of deadly nightshade and poison ivy.

It had been raining in the afternoon, and as I drove up the avenue the mournful dripping of the rain from the dark trees accentuated the cheerlessness of the gloom. The vehicle in which I rode was a fly on three wheels, the fourth having apparently been broken and taken off, causing the fly to sag on one side and drag on its axle over the muddy ground, the fly thus moving only at a foot's pace in a way calculated to enhance the dreariness of the occasion. The driver on the box in front of me was so thickly muffled up as to be undistinguishable, while the horse which drew us was so thickly coated with mist as to be practically invisible. Seldom, I may say, have I had a drive of so mournful a character.

The avenue presently opened out upon a lawn with overgrown shrubberies and in the half darkness I could see the outline of the Grange itself, a rambling, dilapidated building. A dim light struggled through the casement of a window in a tower room. Save for the melancholy cry of a row of owls sitting on the roof, and croaking of the frogs in the moat which ran around the grounds, the place was soundless. My driver halted his horse at the hither side of the moat. I tried in vain to urge him, by signs, to go further. I could see by the fellow's face that he was in a paroxysm of fear and indeed nothing but the extra sixpence which I had added to his fare would have made him undertake the drive up the avenue. I had no sooner alighted than he wheeled his cab about and made off.

Laughing heartily at the fellow's trepidation (I have a way of laughing heartily in the dark), I made my way to the door and pulled the bell-handle. I could hear the muffled reverberations of the bell far within the building. Then all was silent. I bent my ear to listen, but could hear nothing except perhaps the sound of a low moaning as of a person in pain or in great mental distress. Convinced, however, from what my friend Sir Jeremy Buggam had told me, that the Grange was not empty, I raised the ponderous knocker and beat with it loudly against the door.

But perhaps at this point I may do well to explain to my readers (before they are too frightened to listen to me) how I came to be beating on the door of Buggam Grange at nightfall on a gloomy November evening.

A year before I had been sitting with Sir Jeremy Buggam, the present baronet, on the verandah of his ranch in California.

"So you don't believe in the supernatural?" he was saying.

"Not in the slightest," I answered, lighting a cigar as I spoke. When I want to speak very positively, I generally light a cigar as I speak.

"Well, at any rate, Digby," said Sir Jeremy, "Buggam Grange is haunted. If you want to be assured of it go down there any time and spend the night and you'll see for yourself."

"My dear fellow," I replied, "nothing will give me greater pleasure. I shall be back in England in six weeks, and I shall be delighted to put your ideas to the test. Now tell me," I added somewhat cynically, "is there any particular season or day when your Grange is supposed to be specially terrible?"

Sir Jeremy looked at me strangely. "Why do you ask that?" he said. "Have you heard the story of the Grange?"

"Never heard of the place in my life," I answered cheerily, "till you mentioned it to-night, my dear fellow, I hadn't the remotest idea that you still owned property in England."

"The Grange is shut up," said Sir Jeremy, "and has been for twenty years. But I keep a man there – Horrod – he was butler in my father's time and before. If you care to go, I'll write him that you're coming. And since you are taking your own fate in your hands, the fifteenth of November is the day."

At that moment Lady Buggam and Clara and the other girls came trooping out on the verandah, and the whole thing passed clean out of my mind. Nor did I think of it again until I was back in London. Then by one of those strange coincidences or premonitions – call it what you will – it suddenly occurred to me one morning that it was the fifteenth of November. Whether Sir Jeremy had written to Horrod or not, I did not know. But none the less nightfall found me, as I have described, knocking at the door of Buggam Grange.

The sound of the knocker had scarcely ceased to echo when I heard the shuffling of feet within, and the sound of chains and bolts being withdrawn. The door opened. A man stood before me holding a lighted candle which he shaded with his hand. His faded black clothes, once apparently a butler's dress, his white hair and advanced age left me in no doubt that he was Horrod of whom Sir Jeremy had spoken.

Without a word he motioned me to come in, and, still without speech, he helped me to remove my wet outer garments, and then beckoned me into a great room, evidently the dining room of the Grange.

I am not in any degree a nervous man by temperament, as I think I remarked before, and yet there was something in the vastness of the wainscotted room, lighted only by a single candle, and in the silence of the empty house, and still more in the appearance of my speechless attendant which gave me a feeling of distinct uneasiness. As Horrod moved to and fro I took occasion to scrutinize his face more narrowly. I have seldom seen features more calculated to inspire a nervous dread. The pallor of his face and the whiteness of his hair (the man was at least seventy), and still more the peculiar furtiveness of his eyes, seemed to mark him as one who lived under a great terror. He moved with a noiseless step and at times he turned his head to glance in the dark corners of the room.

"Sir Jeremy told me," I said, speaking as loudly and as heartily as I could, "that he would apprise you of my coming."

I was looking into his face as I spoke.

In answer Horrod laid his finger across his lips and I knew that he was deaf and dumb. I am not nervous (I think I said that), but the realization that my sole companion in the empty house was a deaf mute struck a cold chill to my heart.

Horrod laid in front of me a cold meat pie, a cold goose, a cheese, and a tall flagon of cider. But my appetite was gone. I ate the goose, but found that after I had finished the pie I had but little zest for the cheese, which I finished without enjoyment. The cider had a sour taste, and after having permitted Horrod to refill the flagon twice, I found that it induced a sense of melancholy and decided to drink no more.

My meal finished, the butler picked up the candle and beckoned to me to follow him. We passed through the empty corridors of the house, a long line of pictured Buggams looking upon us as we passed, their portraits in the flickering light of the taper assuming a strange and life-like appearance as if leaning forward from their frames to gaze upon the intruder.

Horrod led me upstairs and I realized that he was taking me to the tower in the east wing in which I had observed a light.

The rooms to which the butler conducted me consisted of a sitting room with an adjoining bedroom, both of them fitted with antique wainscotting against which a faded tapestry fluttered. There was a candle burning on the table in the sitting room but its insufficient light only rendered the surroundings the more dismal. Horrod bent down in front of the fireplace and endeavoured to light a fire there. But the wood was evidently damp, and the fire flickered feebly on the hearth.

The butler left me, and in the stillness of the house I could hear his shuffling step echo down the corridor. It may have been fancy, but it seemed to me that his departure was the signal for a low moan that came from somewhere behind the wainscot. There was a narrow cupboard door at one side of the room, and for the moment I wondered whether the moaning came from within. I am not as a rule lacking in courage (I am sure my reader will be decent enough to believe this), yet I found myself entirely unwilling to open the cupboard door and look within. In place of doing so I seated myself in a great chair in front of the feeble fire. I must have been seated there for some time when I happened to lift my eyes to the mantel above and saw, standing upon it, a letter addressed to myself. I knew the handwriting at once to be that of Sir Jeremy Buggam.

I opened it, and spreading it out within reach of the feeble candle light, I read as follows:

"My dear Digby,

In our talk that you will remember I had no time to finish telling you about the mystery of Buggam Grange. I take for granted, however, that you will go there and that Horrod will put you in the tower rooms, which are the only ones that make any pretense of being habitable. I have, therefore, sent him this letter to deliver at the Grange itself. The story is this:

On the night of the fifteenth of November, fifty years ago, my grandfather was murdered in the room in which you are sitting, by his cousin Sir Duggam Buggam. He was stabbed from behind while seated at the little table at which you are probably reading this letter. The two had been playing cards at the table and my grandfather's body was found lying in a litter of cards and gold sovereigns on the floor. Sir Duggam Buggam, insensible from drink, lay beside him, the fatal knife at his hand, his fingers smeared with blood. My grandfather, though of the younger branch, possessed a part of the estates which were to revert to Sir Duggam on his death. Sir Duggam Buggam was tried at the Assizes and was hanged. On the day of his execution he was permitted by the authorities, out of respect for his rank, to wear a mask to the scaffold. The clothes in which he was executed are hanging at full length in the little cupboard to your right, and the mask is above them. It is said that on every fifteenth of November at midnight the cupboard door opens and Sir Duggam Buggam walks out into the room. It has been found impossible to get servants to remain at the Grange, and the place – except for the presence of Horrod – has been unoccupied for a generation. At the time of the murder Horrod was a young man of twenty-two, newly entered into the service of the family. It was he who entered the room and discovered the crime. On the day of the execution he was stricken with paralysis and has never spoken since. From that time to this he has never consented to leave the Grange where he lives in isolation.

Wishing you a pleasant night after your tiring journey,

I remain,

Very faithfully,

JEREMY BUGGAM."

I leave my reader to imagine my state of mind when I completed the perusal of the letter.

I have as little belief in the supernatural as anyone, yet I must confess that there was something in the surroundings in which I now found myself which rendered me at least uncomfortable. My reader may smile if he will, but I assure him that it was with a very distinct feeling of uneasiness that I at length managed to rise to my feet, and, grasping my candle in my hand, to move backward into the bedroom. As I backed into it something so like a moan seemed to proceed from the closed cupboard that I accelerated my backward movement to a considerable degree. I hastily blew out the candle, threw myself upon the bed and drew the bed clothes over my head, keeping, however, one eye and one ear still out and available.

How long I lay thus listening to every sound, I cannot tell. The stillness had become absolute. From time to time I could dimly hear the distant cry of an owl and once far away in the building below a sound as of someone dragging a chain along a floor. More than once I was certain that I heard the sound of moaning behind the wainscot. Meantime I realized that the hour must now be drawing close upon the fatal moment of midnight. My watch I could not see in the darkness, but by reckoning the time that must have elapsed I knew that midnight could not be far away. Then presently my ear, alert to every sound, could just distinguish far away across the fens the striking of a church bell, in the clock tower of Buggam village church, no doubt, tolling the hour of twelve.

On the last stroke of twelve, the cupboard door in the next room opened. There is no need to ask me how I knew it. I couldn't, of course, see it, but I could hear, or sense in some way, the sound of it. I could feel my hair, all of it, rising upon my head. I was aware that there was a *presence* in the adjoining room, I will not say a person, a living soul, but a *presence*. Anyone who has been in the next room to a presence will know just how I felt. I could hear a sound as of someone groping on the floor and the faint rattle as of coins.

My hair was now perpendicular. My reader can blame it or not, but it was.

Then at this very moment from somewhere below in the building there came the sound of a prolonged and piercing cry, a cry as of a soul passing in agony. My reader may censure me or not, but right at this moment I decided to beat it. Whether I should have remained to see what was happening is a question that I will not discuss. My one idea was to get out and to get out quickly. The window of the tower room was some twenty-five feet above the ground. I sprang out through the casement in one leap and landed on the grass below. I jumped over the shrubbery in one bound and cleared the moat in one jump. I went down the avenue in about six strides and ran five miles along the road through the fens in three minutes. This at least is an accurate transcription of my sensations. It may have taken longer. I never stopped till I found myself on the threshold of the Buggam Arms in Little Buggam, beating on the door for the landlord.

I returned to Buggam Grange on the next day in the bright sunlight of a frosty November morning, in a seven cylinder motor car with six local constables and a physician. It makes all the difference. We carried revolvers, spades, pickaxes, shotguns and a ouija board.

What we found cleared up forever the mystery of the Grange. We discovered Horrod the butler lying on the dining room floor quite dead. The physician said that he had died from heart failure. There was evidence from the marks of his shoes in the dust that he had come in the night to the tower room. On the table he had placed a paper which contained a full confession of his having murdered Jeremy Buggam fifty years before. The circumstances of the murder had rendered it easy for him to fasten the crime upon Sir Duggam, already insensible from drink. A few minutes with the ouija board enabled us to get a full corroboration from Sir Duggam. He promised moreover, now that his name was cleared, to go away from the premises forever.

My friend, the present Sir Jeremy, has rehabilitated Buggam Grange. The place is rebuilt. The moat is drained. The whole house is lit with electricity. There are beautiful motor drives in all directions in the woods. He has had the bats shot and the owls stuffed. His daughter, Clara Buggam, became my wife. She is looking over my shoulder as I write. What more do you want?

Up North

Mavis Gallant

When they woke up in the train, their bed was black with soot and there was soot in his Mum's blondie hair. They were miles north of Montreal, which had, already, sunk beneath his remembrance. "D'you know what I sor in the night?" said Dennis. He had to keep his back turned while she dressed. They were both in the same berth, to save money. He was small, and didn't take up much room, but when he woke up in that sooty autumn dawn, he found he was squashed flat against the side of the train. His Mum was afraid of falling out and into the aisle; they had a lower berth, but she didn't trust the strength of the curtain. Now she was dressing, and sobbing; really sobbing. For this was worse than anything she had ever been through, she told him. She had been right through the worst of the air raids, yet this was the worst, this waking in the cold, this dark, dirty dawn, everything dirty she touched, her clothes – oh, her clothes! – and now having to dress as she lay flat on her back. She daren't sit up. She might knock her head.

"You know what I sor?" said the child patiently. "Well, the train must of stopped, see, and some little men with bundles on their backs got on. Other men was holding lanterns. They were all little. They were all talking French."

"Shut up," said Mum. "Do you hear me?"

"Sor them," said the boy.

"You and your bloody elves."

"They was people."

"Little men with bundles," said Mum, trying to dress again. "You start your fairy tales with your Dad and I don't know what *he'll* give you."

It was this mythical, towering, half-remembered figure they were now travelling to join up north.

Roy McLaughlin, travelling on the same train, saw the pair, presently, out of his small red-lidded eyes. Den and his Mum were dressed and as clean as they could make themselves, and sitting at the end of the car. McLaughlin was the last person to get up, and he climbed down from his solitary green-curtained cubicle conspicuous and alone. He had to pad the length of the car in a trench coat and city shoes – he had never owned slippers, bathrobe, or pajamas – past the passengers, who were drawn with fatigue, pale under the lights. They were men, mostly; some soldiers. The Second World War had been finished, in Europe, a year and five months. It was a dirty, rickety train going up to Abitibi. McLaughlin was returning to a construction camp after three weeks in Montreal. He saw the girl, riding with her back to the engine, doing her nails, and his faculties absently registered "Limey bride" as he went by. The kid, looking out the window, turned and stared. McLaughlin thought "Pest," but only because children and other men's wives made him nervous and sour when they were brought around camp on a job.

After McLaughlin had dressed and had swallowed a drink in the washroom – for he was sick and trembling after his holiday – he came and sat down opposite the blond girl. He did not bother to explain that he had to sit somewhere while his berth was being dismantled. His arms were covered with coarse red hair; he had rolled up the sleeves of his khaki shirt. He spread his pale, heavy hands on his knees. The child stood between them, fingertips on the sooty window sill, looking out at the breaking day. Once, the train stopped for a long time; the engine was being changed, McLaughlin said. They had been rolling north but were now turning west. At six o'clock, in about an hour, Dennis and his mother would have to get down, and onto another train, and go north once more. Dennis could not see any station where they were now. There was a swamp with bristling black rushes, red as ink. It was the autumn sunrise; cold, red. It was so strange to him, so singular, that he could not have said an hour later which feature of the scene was in the foreground or to the left or right. Two women wearing army battle jackets over their dresses, with their hair piled up in front, like his mother's, called and giggled to someone they had put on the train. They were fat and dark–grinny. His mother looked at them with detestation, recognizing what they were; for she hated whores. She had always acted on the desire of the moment, without thought of gain, and she had taken the consequences (Dennis) without complaint. Dennis saw that she was hating the women, and so he looked elsewhere. On a wooden fence sat four or five men in open shirts and patched trousers. They had dull, dark hair, and let their mouths sag as though they were too tired or too sleepy to keep them closed. Something about them was displeasing to the child, and he thought that this was an ugly place with ugly people. It was also a dirty place; every time Dennis put his hands on the window sill they came off black.

"Come down any time to see a train go by," said McLaughlin, meaning those men. "Get up in the *night* to see a train."

The train moved. It was still dark enough outside for Dennis to see his face in the window and for the light from the windows to fall in pale squares on the upturned vanishing faces and on the little trees. Dennis heard his mother's new friend say, "Well, there's different possibilities." They passed into an unchanging landscape of swamp and bracken and stunted trees. Then the lights inside the train were put out and he saw that the sky was blue and bright. His mother and McLaughlin, seen in the window, had been remote and bodiless; through their transparent profiles he had seen the yellowed trees going by. Now he could not see their faces at all.

"He's been back in Canada since the end of the war. He was wounded. Den hardly knows him," he heard his mother say. "I couldn't come. I had to wait my turn. We were over a thousand war brides on that ship. He was with Aluminium when he first came back." She pronounced the five vowels in the word.

"You'll be all right there," said McLaughlin. "It's a big place. Schools. All company."

"Pardon me?"

"I mean it all belongs to Aluminum. Only if that's where you're going you happen to be on the wrong train."

"He isn't there now. He hates towns. He seems to move about a great deal. He drives a bulldozer, you see."

"Owns it?" said McLaughlin.

"Why, I shouldn't *think* so. Drives for another man, I think he said."

The boy's father fell into the vast pool of casual labor, drifters; there was a social hierarchy in the north, just as in Heaven. McLaughlin was an engineer. He took another look at the boy; black hair, blue eyes. The hair was coarse, straight, rather dull; Indian hair. The mother was a blonde; touched up a bit, but still blond.

"What name?" said McLaughlin on the upward note of someone who has asked the same question twice.

"Cameron. Donald Cameron."

That meant nothing, still; McLaughlin had worked in a place on James Bay where the Indians were named MacDonald and Ogilvie and had an unconquered genetic strain of blue eyes.

"D'you know about any ghosts?" said the boy, turning to McLaughlin. McLaughlin's eyes were paler than his own, which were a deep slate blue, like the eyes of a newly born child. McLaughlin saw the way he held his footing on the rocking train, putting out a few fingers to the window sill only for the form of the thing. He looked all at once ridiculous and dishonored in his cheap English clothes – the little jacket, the Tweedledum cap on his head. He outdistanced his clothes; he was better than they were. But he was rushing on this train into an existence where his clothes would be too good for him.

"D'you know about any ghosts?" said the boy again.

"Oh, sure," said McLaughlin, and shivered, for he still felt sick, even though he was sharing a bottle with the Limey bride. He said, "Indians see them," which was as close as he could come to being crafty. But there was no reaction out of the mother; she was not English for nothing.

"You seen any?"

"*I'm* not an Indian," McLaughlin started to say; instead he said, "Well, yes, I saw the ghost, or something like the ghost, of a dog I had."

They looked at each other, and the boy's mother said, "Stop that, you two. Stop that this minute."

"I'll tell you a strange thing about Dennis," said his mother. "It's this. There's times he gives me the creeps."

Dennis was lying on the seat beside her with his head on her lap.

She said, "If I don't like it I can clear out. I was a waitress. There's always work."

"Or find another man," McLaughlin said. "Only it won't be me, girlie. I'll be far away."

"Den says that when the train stopped he saw a lot of elves," she said, complaining.

"Not elves – men," said Dennis. "Some of them had mattresses rolled up on their backs. They were little and bent over. They were talking French. They were going up north."

McLaughlin coughed and said, "He means settlers. They were sent up on this same train during the depression. But that's nine, ten years ago. It was supposed to clear the unemployed out of the towns, get them off relief. But there wasn't anything up here then. The winters were terrible. A lot of them died."

"He couldn't know that," said Mum edgily. "For that matter, how can he tell what is French? He's never heard any."

"No, he couldn't know. It was around ten years ago, when times were bad."

"Are they good now?"

"Jeez, after a *war*?" He shoved his hand in the pocket of his shirt, where he kept a roll, and he let her see the edge of it.

She made no comment, but put her hand on Den's head and said to him, "You didn't see anyone. Now shut up."

"Sor 'em," the boy said in a voice as low as he could descend without falling into a whisper.

"You'll see what your Dad'll give you when you tell lies." But she was halfhearted about the threat and did not quite believe in it. She had been attracted to the scenery, whose persistent sameness she could no longer ignore. "It's not proper country," she said. "It's bare."

"Not enough for me," said McLaughlin. "Too many people. I keep on moving north."

"I want to see some Indians," said Dennis, sitting up.

"There aren't any," his mother said. "Only in films."

"I don't like Canada." He held her arm. "Let's go home now."

"It's the train whistle. It's so sad. It gets him down."

The train slowed, jerked, flung them against each other, and came to a stop. It was quite day now; their faces were plain and clear, as if drawn without shading on white paper. McLaughlin felt responsible for them, even compassionate; the change in him made the boy afraid.

"We're getting down, Den," said his Mum, with great, wide eyes. "We take another train. See? It'll be grand. Do you hear what Mum's telling you?"

He was determined not to leave the train, and clung to the window sill, which was too smooth and narrow to provide a grip; McLaughlin had no difficulty getting him away. "I'll give you a present," he said hurriedly. But he slapped all his pockets and found nothing to give. He did not think of the money, and his watch had been stolen in Montreal. The woman and the boy struggled out with their baggage, and McLaughlin, who had descended first so as to help them down, reached up and swung the boy in his arms.

"The Indians!" the boy cried, clinging to the train, to air; to anything. His face was momentarily muffled by McLaughlin's shirt. His cap fell to the ground. He screamed, "Where's Mum? I never saw *any*thing!"

"You saw Indians," said McLaughlin. "On the rail fence, at that long stop. Look, don't worry your mother. Don't keep telling her what you haven't seen. You'll be seeing plenty of everything now."

The Snow Walker

Farley Mowat

I am Ootek, and my people are the people of the River of Men. Once they were many and the land was good to them, but now it is my time and we have almost forgotten how it was in the old days when the deer flooded the tundra and gave us life. Hunger comes often now, and the deer but seldom. No one now lives by the big lakes to the north although when my father was young the tents of the people stood everywhere along those shores. I have travelled down the River to the big lakes but when I reached them I turned back from an empty land.

Only the spirits who remain in those places remember the times when a man might stand on a hill as the deer passed by and though he looked to the east or the west, the south or the north, he would see only their brown backs and hear only the clicking of antlers and the grumbling of their full bellies.

The great herds have gone . . . and so we who lived by the deer must follow the Snow Walker even as my father followed him in the spring of the year.

After the ice had grown thick on the lakes last winter there came a time of storms and for many days we stayed in our igloos. The children grew quiet and did not play and the old people sometimes looked toward the door tunnels with shadowed eyes. The snows mounted over the top of the igloos until we could not even venture out to look for willow twigs to burn. The igloos were cold and dark for we had long since eaten the deer fat that should have burned in the lamps. So little food remained to us from the few southbound deer we had been able to kill in the autumn that the dogs were beginning to starve, and we ourselves were not much better off.

One day Belikari, who was my closest neighbour among the seven families living in the camp, came to tell me that a mad fox had run into the tunnel of his snowhouse where his dogs lay and had bitten three of them before it was killed by the rest. Those three dogs died with foam at their lips, and they were only three of many. This was another evil because when the foxes went mad their pelts became worthless and so, even if the storms had allowed us to travel, it would have been no use visiting the traps.

After a long time the blizzards ended and the weather grew calm and cold. All the people had survived though some of the old ones could hardly stir from the sleeping ledges. We younger men took the few remaining dogs and went searching for meat we had cached on the Flat Country. We found only a little because most of the caches were buried under hard drifts that had mounted so high they had covered the markers.

The women and children helped to keep famine at bay by digging under the drifts near the igloos for fish bones and scraps of old hides with which to make soup. By such means we hoped to cling to our lives until the warm winds and the lengthening days might bring the deer back to our country from the forested lands in the south.

But long after the time when the ice should have started to rot, it still lay heavy and hard on the rivers and lakes, and the days seemed to grow colder again until we wondered if winter would ever come to an end. We ate all the food we had, and the deer did not come. We waited . . . for there was nothing else we could do. We ate the last of our dogs, and still the deer did not come.

One day the men gathered in Owliktuk's snowhouse. His wife, Kunee, sat on the ledge with her child in her arms, and the child was dead. We knew it could not be very long before many of the women were nursing such sorrow. My cousin, Ohoto, put some thoughts into words.

"Perhaps people should go away from this place now. Perhaps they might go south to the place where the white man has come to live. It might happen that he would have food he would give us."

The white man had only recently come to live on the edge of our country, to trade with us for foxes. It was a long way to his place and only Ohoto had been there before. Since we had no dogs, we knew we would have to carry everything on our backs, and the children and old people would not be able to ride on the sleds as they should. We knew some of them would not see the white man's place . . . but the child of Owliktuk and Kunee was dead. We decided to go.

The women rolled up a few skins to use for tent shelters and sleeping robes; the children carried whatever they could, and we men slung our packs on our shoulders and we left our camp by the River and set out into the south.

Soon after we started, the sun turned warm and for five days we walked up to our knees in melting snow. My wife's mother had lost count of the years she had lived, yet she walked with the rest and still helped to pitch camp at the end of each day. But on the fifth night she did not offer to help. She sat by herself with her back to a rock and spoke to none except Ilupalee, my daughter. She called the child to her.

From a distance I watched and listened as the old woman put her bony hands on my daughter's head. I heard her softly singing her spirit song to the child, the secret song she had received from her mother's mother and with which she could summon her helping spirit. Then I knew she had made up her mind what she must do.

It was her choice, and my wife and I could say nothing about it, not even to tell her of the sorrow we felt. During the night, she went from the camp. None saw her go. We did not speak her name after that for one may not use the name of a person who has gone out on the land to seek the Snow Walker until the name and the spirit it bears can be given again to a newly born child.

The next day we reached the Little Stick country which borders the forests. Here there was plenty of wood so we could at least have fires where we could warm ourselves. Toward evening we overtook Ohoto's family squatted beside a fire, melting water to drink since there was no food. Ohoto told me his daughter had fallen and could not rise again so they had to make camp. When the rest of the people came up, it was clear that many, both young and old, could not go on; and Ohoto thought we were still two or three days distant from the home of the white man.

I had been carrying Ilupalee on my shoulders most of the day and was so tired I could not think. I lay down by the fire and shut my eyes. Ilupalee lay beside me and whispered in my ear:

"A white hare is sitting behind the little trees over there."

I thought this was only a dream born out of hunger so I did not open my eyes. But she whispered again:

"It is a big, fat hare. She Who Walked said it was there."

This time I opened my eyes and got to my knees. I looked where she pointed and could see nothing except a patch of dwarf spruce. All the same I unslung the rifle from my pack and walked toward the trees.

Indeed it was there!

But one hare does not provide more than a mouthful of food for twenty-five people so we had to think carefully what should be done. It was decided that the three strongest men —Alekahaw, Ohoto and I—would eat the hare and thereby gain strength to go on to the white man's place. My wife built a fire apart from the camp so the others would not have to endure the smell of meat cooking. She boiled the hare and we three men shared it; but we left the guts, bones, skin and the head to make soup for the children.

We walked away from the camp along a frozen stream so we would not have to wade through the soft snow. My skin boots were thin and torn and my feet were soon numb because at each step we broke through the thin crust above the thaw water. I did not mind because my stomach was warm.

It was growing dark on the second day when we came to a clearing in a spruce woods on the shore of a lake where the white man had his house. His dogs heard us and howled and when we came near he opened the door and waited with the bright light of a lamp shining behind him. We stopped and stood where we were because he was a stranger, and a white man, and we had met very few white men. He spoke to us, but not in our language, so we could not reply. When he spoke again, very loudly, and still we did not reply, he went back into his house.

It grew cold as the darkness settled around us, and our wet boots became stiff as they froze. I thought of Ilupalee and wanted very much to do something, but did not know what we should do.

After a long time the door opened again and the white man came out. He was wiping his beard. We smelled hot fat from his house but he shut the door behind him and motioned us to follow him to another small cabin.

He unlocked the door and we went in. He lit a lamp and hung it on a rafter so we could see that the walls were piled high with boxes, but we looked hardest at the many bags of flour stacked in front of a table. We started to smile for we believed the white man understood our needs and would help us. We stood under the lamp watching the flame reflect light from the beads of cold fat still clinging to the white man's beard, and we gave ourselves up to the joy growing within us.

The white man opened a drawer in the table and took out a handful of small sticks of the kind used to show how much a trapper can have in exchange for the fox pelts he brings. Holding these sticks in his hand he spoke sharply in his own tongue. When we did not reply he went to a wall of the cabin, took down a fox pelt and laid it before us; then he pointed to the carrying bags which were slung on our shoulders.

The joy went out of us then. I made signs to show we had no fox pelts to trade, and Alekahaw opened his bag to show how empty it was. The white man's eyes were of a strange green colour and I could not look into them. I looked at his forehead instead while I waited for whatever must happen. Slowly his face grew red with anger, then he threw the sticks back in the drawer and began to shout at us.

Anger is something we fear since an angry man may do foolish and dangerous things. When I saw the anger in this man's face, I backed to the door. I wanted to go from that place but Alekahaw was braver than me. He stood where he was and tried to explain to the white man how it was at the camp where the rest of the people were starving. He pulled up his *holiktu* so the man could see for himself how Alekahaw's ribs stuck out from his body. Alekahaw touched his own face to show how tightly the skin was stretched over the bones.

The white man shrugged his shoulders. Perhaps he did not understand. He began turning down the flame in the lamp and we knew he would soon go back to his house, then the door would be shut against the needs of the people. Quickly Ohoto pulled two boxes of shells out of his bag. These were the last bullets he had and he had been saving them against the time when the deer would return. Now he put them on the table and pointed to the flour.

The white man shook his head. He was still angry. He picked up the lamp and started to go to the door. Alekahaw and Ohoto stepped out of his way, but something happened inside me and although I was frightened I would not let him pass.

He kept his eyes on me but he stretched out one hand behind him until it came to rest on a rifle hung on the wall. I could not make way for him then because I was afraid to move while he had his hand on that gun.

So we all stood still for a while. At last he picked up a small sack of flour and threw it over the table to fall at Ohoto's feet. Then he took the rifle, shoved me aside with the barrel, pushed the door open and told us to leave. We went outside and watched as he locked the door. We watched as he went back into his house.

A little while later we saw him looking out of his window. He still had the rifle in his hand so we knew there was no use remaining. We walked away into the darkness.

Day was breaking when we got back to the camp. Those who were still able to stand gathered in front of Owliktuk's tent and we told what we had to tell. We showed them the sack of flour which was so small a child could easily lift it.

Owliktuk spoke against us, blaming us because we had not taken the food that was needed. He said we could have repaid the white man next winter when the foxes were again good. But if we had tried to take food from the white man there would have been killing. Perhaps Owliktuk only spoke as he did because his second child was now going from him. The rest of the people said nothing but returned to their families with the small portions of flour which were their shares.

I carried my father's share to his tent. Although he had once been the best hunter among us and only the previous year had fathered a child on his third wife, he had aged very much during the winter and his legs had weakened until he could barely walk. When I told him what had happened and gave him the flour for himself, my stepmother and the small child, he smiled and said, "One has a son who knows what may be done and what may not be done. One is glad no blood was shed. It may be that things will get better."

It did not seem he was right about that. We had made the journey to the white man's place and it had come to so little. Now we were too weak to go back to our own land. And on the second day after we three men returned to the camp, the Snow Walker came to the children Aljut and Uktilohik. There was no mourning for them because those who still lived had no sorrow to spend on the dead.

Each day thereafter the sun shone more brightly. Spring was upon us and still the deer had not returned. One day I tried to visit my father to see how it was with him but I was unable to walk that short distance. I crawled back into my own tent where my wife sat rocking herself with her eyes closed and her mouth wide and gasping. Beside her my daughter sometimes wailed in the thin, dry voice of an old woman. I lay down on some brush inside the flap and together we waited.

Perhaps it was the next day when I awakened to hear someone shout. The shout came again and the voice seemed familiar and the words set my heart racing.

"Here is a deer!"

I caught my rifle by the muzzle and crawled into the morning sunlight. At first I was blinded but after a moment I saw a fine buck standing a little way off with his head high, watching the camp.

I raised my rifle with hands that could not seem to hold it. The sights wavered and the deer seemed to slide up and down the barrel. Clutching it tight, I took aim and fired. The buck flung up his forefeet and leapt toward the sheltering trees. I fired again and again until the rifle was empty but the shots all went wide. I could see them kicking up little spouts of snow but I could not hear the hard thud that tells a hunter when he has hit.

The deer ran away . . . but just when it was about to disappear in the trees it stumbled and fell. With all my strength I willed it not to get up. The deer's spirit struggled with mine until slowly the buck sank on his side.

Some of the people had come out into the sunlight and with weak voices were asking each other who had been shooting.

"Get out your knives!" I cried as loud as I could. "One has killed a fat deer!"

At my words even those who could not walk found enough strength. People wept as they stumbled and staggered toward the deer carcass. The first ones to reach it clung to it like flies, sucking the blood that still bubbled out of its wound. They moved away after a while to make room for others, sobbing with pain and holding their hands to their bellies.

The women sliced into the carcass with their round knives and tore out the entrails, snatching at the little scraps of white fat that clung to the guts. The men cut off the legs at the lower joints and cracked the bones to get at the marrow. In only a short time the buck was changed into a pile of bones, steaming meat and red snow.

It grew warm under the sun and some people began returning to the shelters with meat for those who were too weak to move. Then I remembered that I had seen no one from the tent of my father, so I made my way there dragging part of a forequarter. The flap was down over the door but I pushed it aside and crawled in. My stepmother was lying under a piece of hairless old hide and she was holding her child against her dry dugs. Although they scarcely breathed they were both still alive. But of my father there was no sign.

I cut off a piece of meat, chewed it soft then pushed it into my stepmother's mouth and rubbed her neck till she swallowed. Then I took my little stepbrother to Ohoto's shelter, which was not far away, and Ohoto's wife made blood soup and fed the child with it while I went back to my father's place and chewed more meat for my stepmother. Before I left her, she was able to eat by herself but she could not yet talk so I did not know where my father had gone.

When I returned to my own place, I found my wife had roasted some ribs and boiled the deer's tongue. Ilupalee lay wrapped in a fresh piece of deerskin and it was good to hear her whimper with the pain of a full belly. That whole night we passed in eating and by the next day nothing of the buck remained for the ravens and foxes. The bones had been crushed and boiled for their fat, the skull had been opened and cleaned, and even the hooves had been made into soup. The strength of the buck had passed into the people and we were ready to return to our country.

Next day when I went to my father's tent my stepmother was able to stand. I told her that she and the child would now come and live in my tent, then I said, "One looks about but does not see one's father."

"Eeee," she replied. "He would not eat the flour you brought. He gave it to me and the child. Afterwards he went on the land to meet the Snow Walker."

A little while later I told Ohoto about the voice I had heard. No one else had heard it and none of the people in the camp except me had known there was a deer nearby. Together Ohoto and I followed the marks where my father had stumbled down to the river, then crawled north on the ice. His tracks disappeared at a bend where the current had opened a hole, but close by we found the tracks of a deer. We followed the tracks until they circled back to the camp and came to an end at the place where I had killed the big buck. Neither Ohoto nor I said anything but we both knew whose voice I had heard.

In the autumn my wife will give birth to another child, and then the name of him who went to meet the Snow Walker that we might continue to live will surely be spoken again by the River of Men.

The Timeless Island

H. R. Percy

Joan and Edgar scrambled ashore under the disapproving eye of the skipper, a little man with an aggressively poised chin and a forbidding cast to his eye. He had made it clear that he did not make a practice of carrying mere sightseers in his boat, and had hinted in a sinister manner that if they were not ready to step aboard when he called on his return trip, he would find great satisfaction in leaving them on the island for three days.

The boat swung away almost before they were clear, and made off round the headland with a derisive hoot. They were left with a sudden sense of loneliness amid immensity. The lapping of the sea seemed only to emphasize a silence into which their footfalls on the planks broke with disconcerting echoes. A flock of gulls rose from the rocks in raucous protest, and settled uneasily at a distance as these alien creatures invaded their peace.

Edgar looked about him, still misty-eyed with remembering, at widely scattered crofts and the tiny isolated kirk set like a watch-tower on the shoulder of the hill.

"That's the site of the old camp up there," he said, pointing. "Not much sign of it now. Care to have a look?"

"All right." Even Joan's tact could not instil enthusiasm into her acquiescence. She had begun to suspect that Edgar's urge to revisit Dunkelvie arose from no more than a nostalgic impulse. The preposterous thought even crossed her mind that the whole concept of their tour, planned and improved upon through the long Ontario winter, had been founded upon a secret yearning of Edgar's to come back here. He was capable of that. A place like this would appeal to his imagination; the wide expanses, the restful contours, the sunlit sweeps of heather, and the soothing sense of a host of tomorrows waiting to be lived without haste or calculation. Of friends, it was sufficient that they lived and were in accord with one, but familiar places tugged relentlessly, dangling promises of resurrected experience. She had not been married to Edgar for a year without discovering his profound sentimentality, and learning to make allowances for it. All the same, an army camp was hardly a place to yearn for, much less to make a pilgrimage to.

Of course, there would have been comrades, but Edgar could surely have re-established contact with them, had he cared. A woman, perhaps? She thrust the thought impatiently aside and bent to pick a spray of flowers growing at the side of the path. This was no day, and she was in no mood, for a conducted tour. She felt girlish and inconsequent. For her there was sufficient pleasure to be found in wandering and gathering flowers, and letting the spirit of the place seep into her.

If Edgar once persuaded himself that she was interested, he would be devastatingly eloquent.

"I suppose you are wondering why I wanted to come back here?"

She looked up. So there was a story! Despite his nonchalance he was obviously agog with it. She could sense it surging up within him in response to the influence of the place.

"It did cross my mind," she said.

"It's not an easy thing to explain, even to myself." His eyes ranged the island thoughtfully. "Certain things happened here which I didn't question very deeply at the time. Things perhaps better forgotten. But I couldn't forget. I tried to think the thing out, but in Kitchener it all seemed so irrational. And the more I puzzled over it, the more I wanted to come back here, to convince myself that my imagination had not been running away with me.

"You know, Joan, this is not quite the Dunkelvie I remember." The softly spoken words seemed to dissolve in the silence about them. Joan showed surprise.

"Oh, topographically it's the same. The crofts are the same as they've been for centuries, and no doubt the people are, too. Left alone, they would carry on their way of life to the end of time; life is the only gauge they have of time.

"You can have no idea what this place is like in winter. The greyness of it, and the perpetual damp. No wonder the crofters built their houses with walls like fortresses; the damp used to eat its way into those huts of ours as if they had been made of blotting paper. The mist would close about us without warning, billowing in from the sea like the smoke of some colossal fire, and it would hang about for days, as though it couldn't shake itself free of the spiky heather stalks. Then a wind would spring up, and it would be so cold that we wished the mist back again. The rain came on those winds like icy claws tearing at your face."

They had turned aside from the path and were approaching a broad expanse of blooming heather, sloping gently up and presenting a purple shoulder to the sky. Joan exclaimed at the beauty of it.

"Here," said Edgar, putting the full irony of it into his tone, "is where the camp stood."

"But there's nothing left," Joan said. "Did they pull it down?"

"I really don't know, but if the army didn't, either the islanders or the elements would. The people of Dunkelvie would have been only too pleased when the wind carried away the last trace of our occupation."

"Why?"

"I suppose it was an instinctive dislike. If you tackled them about it, no doubt they would give you a lengthy catalogue of our sins – tell you that we played heathen music on the sabbath, and played at cards, and whistled after their daughters, and generally stood host to the Devil–but it went deeper than that, much deeper."

As they walked, both were searching for some evidence, some trifling memorial of a phase in Edgar's life, but they found none.

"You know well enough, Joan," he said, turning to look into her eyes, "that I'm not one to get bored easily. Give me a book and I could be happy in prison, yet during that winter here there were times when I found myself making the most morbid speculations about the purpose of life. All the books had been so thoroughly read and talked over that we knew their characters as well as we knew each other, and they got on our nerves to about the same degree.

"You can imagine, then, how welcome McCleod was. It was in that period of ultra-boredom following the somewhat forced excitement of Christmas and New Year. I was gazing idly out of the mess window when McCleod was cast up, as it were, out of the sea, and stood shivering on the jetty. Even against the immensity of the sea he looked vast: it reminded me of a picture I once saw of Gulliver surveying the shores of Lilliput.

"I went down to meet him. He stood there looking about him, and as I drew near I could hear that he was humming one of those mournful Scottish airs–the kind that always seems to me to be full of disquieting associations.

"My voice startled him. His eyes were wild, in that moment, as if the words had come out of the air. He looked around him quickly and fixed me at last with a look of relief.

"Come to join us?" I asked him again. He said yes, he had (with a pardonable lack of enthusiasm), and introduced himself in a rich highland accent as James Cameron McCleod. As we walked back to the camp he kept gazing from croft to croft in that strange preoccupied way of his, and I found it difficult to get a word out of him.

"He was a fine-looking fellow. You could imagine him standing on a rock and brandishing a claymore in the face of an advancing army. But a very brief acquaintance was sufficient to dispel that illusion. He was too sensitive to be heroic in that way. I'm not suggesting that he was a coward. Courage was a quality very little in demand in our situation, but I would say from the way in which McCleod faced up to the rigours of Dunkelvie that if he had courage, it was of the passive sort. His was the spirit of martyrdom rather than of rebellion."

On Joan's suggestion they spread Edgar's raincoat on the heather and sat down to eat the sandwiches she had brought. For a time Edgar's narrative was punctuated by rustlings of paper and periods of silent application.

"It's always struck me as queer that McCleod and I should have got on so well together." Edgar pondered it during the mastication of a whole sandwich.

"You see, perhaps the secret was in my readiness to take him seriously. I think Mac's difficulty was that he wanted desperately to appear normal, but at the same time there was another side of his nature that demanded expression. A sort of mysticism, I suppose you'd call it.

"You can imagine how the average soldier would shy away from that sort of thing.

"For the first week or so he was popular enough, but when the novelty wore off and he began to corner the guys one by one and quote outlandish poetry, and sound their opinions on matters like spiritualism and reincarnation, they dropped him as if he'd been a leper."

He reached for another sandwich and studied it with profound concentration. Joan watched him closely, held by the sincerity of his manner. He spoke as if her reception of the story was a matter of vital importance.

"He interested me. It was obvious that he was no crank, and it seemed illogical that an intelligent man should pursue such morbid interests.

"I suppose it was my curiosity, coupled with my readiness to take him seriously, that drew him to me. And as I got to know him it became apparent there was something on his mind.

"We were alone in the mess one Sunday afternoon. The others had been driven to their beds by sheer boredom. I rather fancied myself as a painter in those days, and I decided to take advantage of the quiet to put the finishing touches to a still life I had been striving to master for several weeks. McCleod stood behind me and watched, making an occasional comment. Just by way of conversation I asked him what he thought of Dunkelvie.

"He took it up almost eagerly. 'You know,' he said, strolling across to the window (he had a habit of conversing with his back to the listener), 'you know, there's something queer about this place. Something I don't understand.'

"I said nothing. After all, we all felt that way about it. But he went on to tell me that Dunkelvie was as familiar to him as if he had lived there for years. 'As soon as I saw it on the horizon I knew it; recognized its shape,' he said. 'Couldna take my eyes off it. I knew exactly what to expect as we came round the point; the crofts, the kirk, the very rocks on the shore.'

"I suggested that perhaps he had seen a picture of it somewhere, but he waved the idea aside impatiently."

Edgar leaned back on his elbow and gazed up into Joan's eyes with profound earnestness, anxious, it seemed, to impress upon her the importance of all this.

"What he said was: 'I think I've lived before.'

"I straightened up. McCleod's back was still squarely turned, and he stood there with a forced nonchalance as if disowning so preposterous a statement. I returned to my work and said nothing; but the words had thrown between us a curtain of embarrassment which kept us silent the whole afternoon.

"He began to show an interest in painting, and more for the sake of the distraction than from the hope of worthwhile results, I gave him a few simple lessons. The brush in his great fur-backed hand seemed to have no more artistic potentiality than a skewer through a joint of beef. Yet he made surprisingly rapid progress.

"It wasn't long before I realized that he had the makings of a real painter, and the urge was obviously so strong within him that eventually I withdrew quietly into the background and left him to it. There was nothing further I could teach him, and he was making better use of the canvas than I could ever hope to do.

"In February, after a frost or two, we enjoyed a brief, premature spring. Mac took to painting in the open. His work was purely experimental, and he usually came back morose and frowning, complaining of his inability to get down on canvas what was in his mind, as if that was a curse peculiar to him.

"His pictures lacked something vital—conviction, inspiration, what you will. And the repeated frustration seemed to prey upon him, darkening his countenance and his mind.

"I saw him often standing inert and pensive before the easel. Sometimes I passed quite close—close enough to inspect a blank or a defaced canvas—and he never spared me a glance. The others saw him too, and twitted him with seeking inspiration; but I had already begun to suspect that he was chasing phantoms.

"Then one afternoon I saw him from a distance, working with fervent, almost passionate concentration. He jabbed at the palette as if he begrudged the time spent in replenishing his brush. His easel—a crude affair knocked up out of packing cases—was set up in a hollow between two of the guns. Down there."

Edgar pointed down the seaward slope, and Joan, following the line of his arm, saw a shallow depression with one side dropping sheer to the sea.

"Just about where you see that puddle shining in the sun. I say, that's queer! Water lying on the peat, like that. I wonder if—" The speculation was never uttered. Edgar stood up abruptly and brushed a crumb or two from his jacket. While Joan packed away the debris of their meal he lit his pipe and stood smoking thoughtfully.

"I couldn't imagine why he should choose such a spot. There is a view of the sea, it's true, but it's by no means the best view. As I watched, however, I noticed that his eyes never left the canvas.

"When I came that way three hours later he was still painting frenziedly, regardless of the passing of time and the chilling dampness of the air. It was the failing light that eventually broke through his preoccupation. He returned to the mess looking pale, empty-eyed, and emotionally exhausted.

"For several days all his leisure was passed at that spot,

sometimes painting feverishly, sometimes in a sort of coma. If you spoke to him he would start as if awakened from sleep.

"The fruit of McCleod's brief afflatus was the portrait of a young woman. Perhaps in the niceties of execution it fell short of his earlier efforts, but for sheer vitality and boldness I have seldom seen it equalled.

"Yet there was something undefined about it. It was at the same time vivid and vague, like a dream, or a reflection in water not quite still. There were unexpected lights and shadows, unlooked-for vagaries of colour, which somehow combined to unsettle me.

"The subject of the picture was handsome enough, with very dark, appealing eyes and fine waist-long tresses cascading about her shoulders. But I would not have lived with that picture for the world. I could not have been in the same room without being aware all the time of its soft, imploring gaze following me with a sort of spectral intensity. The background was of frigid green – a mere limbo – so that the face appeared to float just beneath the surface of an icy pool. The chill seemed to communicate itself to the atmosphere, and I felt it creeping into my very bones.

"I turned away from it with a shudder and went to the fire where Mac sat shivering, casting an immense, Buddha-like shadow. He got up hastily, put away the picture, and came back to expose himself greedily to the flames.

" 'It's a masterpiece,' I said, 'no doubt of that.'

"He continued to gaze into the fire without comment, seeming neither glad of my praise nor skeptical of it. He looked limp, played out. 'What I can't understand,' I said, 'is what made you do it.'

"His brow glistened in the firelight, and his hands were clenched tight. How plainly I can see him crouching there, with that great shadow hovering behind as if it gloated over him.

" 'I couldn't help myself,' he told me. 'It's not really my picture at all. I only painted what I saw. And once I began, I couldn't stop.'

"Although his fingers were stiff, and his arm ached, and he was frozen to the bone, he had to go on. When it was all over, he said, it was like starting from a doze; and there was the picture–a tantalizing fragment of a forgotten dream.

"But who was she? I wanted to know. I was half-prepared for his reply, but the look by which it was accompanied appalled me.

" 'Ah! Who is she? I'd give anything in the world to know,' he said. 'Anything. She's out of the past. Out of an earlier life.'

"What, he kept saying, had she to do with him? If only he could remember! But always it just eluded him."

They walked on in silence for some time. Joan, with the sun warm upon her cheek, emerged for a moment from the mesmeric chill into which Edgar's words and her own imagination had plunged her, and darted aside to add to her nosegay.

It was another change in his tone that brought her to heel.

"About that time there was a period of intense activity. The camp shook off its winter lethargy and began preparations for the visit of a Cabinet Minister, who was touring the outposts of defence. Night and day aircraft tested our alertness, and the island shook under our practice fire. Hour after hour during those chilly nights our searchlights scoured the darkness. And it rained incessantly until the peaty soil yielded to the tread like a sodden sponge.

"It was towards the end of one of those night exercises. I was making a last tour of the sites, following roughly the line we are following now. The searchlights had gone out, and the beam of my flashlight cut through the slanting rain and struck a glistening oval before me on the wet, quaggy heather. The rain pattered on my cape incessantly with a rhythm that had a lulling effect on my mind."

He stopped by the pool they had seen from higher up the slope. There was an odd suggestion of solemnity in his pose.

"I was midway between the last two guns–somewhere here–when I saw it. A white object thrusting up out of the heather. Something shockingly familiar in outline. Something alien and awful at such a time and place. I bent closer to look.

"It was–" he glanced quickly at Joan with mingling relish and apology. "It was a human hand. A woman's hand, I judged, held aloft aimlessly; and around it in all directions the heather grew even and undisturbed as a carpet."

"Edgar!" Joan had no clear idea what the exclamation was intended to convey, but something of her inward shudder went into it, and she saw it register on Edgar's pensive face.

"Whatever did you do?" she asked quickly.

"I shouted to raise the alarm. While I stood here listening to the voices approaching through the darkness, the implications of my discovery began to crowd upon me. The hand implied a body, and a body in such a place implied murder. But who? By whom?

"The tide of activity swept over me," he went on. "They came with spades and planks and set to with a great deal of chatter. McCleod came and stood beside me, gripping my arm painfully as he watched the exhumation. As it grew lighter I could see that his face was haggard and grey.

"By the time the diggers had finished their work it was almost daylight. They lifted out a pallid shape, flecked brown with peat, and lowered it onto the heather.

"Where the rain had washed it clean, the body showed not a blemish, not a scar. It was like a sculpture in fine ivory, graceful and—and sublime.

" 'Anyone know who she is?' I remember someone asking. Mac stirred beside me, but said nothing. His eyes were fixed on the still face of the girl with a strange, questioning look; and when I looked in the same direction a cold thrill of recognition passed through me. The same face, the same hair, damp and disordered now; the same disquieting pallor, and something of that same suggestion of unreality.

"Then I remembered him standing there painting, on that very spot. 'I only painted in what I saw,' he had said. And I remembered the look of torment on his face the day he finished the picture. He had been extremely preoccupied ever since that day. His behaviour alone would have been sufficient, when cool heads began to consider, to lay him open to suspicion.

"But there was an unexpected development.

"Naturally, every effort was made to establish the identity of the girl. Visits were made to all the crofts and a sort of census taken of the population. The crofters were of little practical help, but they all dropped hints of a knowledge they did not care to share with us. One or two of them did unbend, though, so far as to say that she was a suicide who had been refused burial in the kirkyard.

"Their confounded indifference blocked our inquiries more effectively than downright lying could have done, and I doubt if the startling fact which transformed the whole affair would ever have come to light if it hadn't been for McCleod's obsession.

"During our house-to-house check-up, it had fallen to Mac to visit a lonely croft on the remote side of the island. We shall shortly come in sight of it. It was managed by an ancient crone and her half-witted son.

"He told me he had never been more certain of anything in his life, than that he had been in that house before. He didn't glean much from that first interview, but something convinced him that there, if anywhere, the solution to the mystery lay, and he resolved to go back and get to the bottom of it."

Edgar, as they came at that moment round a large, naked outcrop, pointed ahead, where the cottage of which he spoke rose in squat silhouette. Above it a thread of peat smoke climbed into the sultry sky.

"There it is. I wonder who keeps it now. The old woman would be dead by this time, of course, and I can't imagine the son running the place alone.

"They were a queer pair. McCleod took me with him when he went again. In the meantime the body had been reburied, and we all shared in the fervent hope that we had seen and heard the last of it. All, that is, except McCleod. He was as anxious to solve the puzzle as we were to forget it.

"Well, he managed to talk me into coming to this croft with him, although it was a damp and bitterly cold night. He was carrying a package which I had little difficulty in identifying as that creepy picture of his, with which he hoped to surprise the old girl into talking.

"You can see that the door is pretty solid. Mac announced our arrival by a lusty kick with his army-size twelve. The door opened a few degrees with uncanny silence and from the crack a face peered out – the most puckered face I have ever seen. A pair of faded eyes looked us over cynically. I heard Mac's boots scraping uneasily on the patch of shingle before the door."

They were now quite close to the cottage.

"To my surprise," Edgar went on, "the crone opened the door wide and shuffled into the gloom beyond. We hesitated for a moment and then followed her in. McCleod ducked low and literally filled the doorway with his great bulk. The woman disposed herself with painful care on a crude, high-backed chair. She pointed across the hearth to a long chest, polished black by generations of uneasy sitters. We sat down like a couple of penitent children, and waited.

"The room was lit only by a small lamp with a blackened glass, and the red glow of the peats. It was very small, yet even coming in from the total darkness I found it difficult to distinguish all the objects in it. The old woman's son sat on a stool in the darkest corner, watching with eyes that glowed out at us like an animal's.

"Most of the floor space was taken up by a scrubbed table and a bed. I suppose the walls had once been whitewashed, but they were now slate-grey, and in the region of the hearth almost black. Overhead was a dark cavity crossed by rafters on which hung the provisions and utensils of the household.

"The silence of those first few minutes had a stifled quality about it. Afterwards I put it down to the fact that there wasn't a clock in the place, but at the time it was eerie enough.

"Mac began to stammer out an apology for our intrusion, but she cut him short by saying she'd expected us, or she'd have been abed hours ago. 'Ye've come about Maggie,' she said.

" 'Is Maggie the name of the girl we found buried in the peat?' I asked. I was anxious to get it over and get away from the place. She said, rather curtly, that she knew of only one being buried loose in Dunkelvie.

"McCleod began to unwrap his parcel.

"She interlaced her fleshless fingers and swayed in her chair. When Mac held up the picture so that the glow of the peat fell on it, she studied it closely.

" 'I mind they used to say the queen was pretty and black-eyed; and my mother used to weep when she combed my bonnie black hair, and say it was just like poor Maggie's.' There was a tear in her own eye as she pointed at the long tresses in the picture. She took off her starched cap, and I saw with an eerie shock that she was quite bald.

" 'Maggie was my mother's sister.' She paused, as if remembering something. 'He painted Maggie's picture, too,' she said. She stood up and shuffled across the room, holding up the lamp to throw light on a picture on the wall. We went to look. The canvas was dark with age, and its subject was barely distinguishable, but beneath the grime I thought I saw a more conventional version of McCleod's picture. McCleod said 'Ah!'

"Maggie, the old woman went on to tell us, was the bonniest lass in Dunkelvie. She was always blithe as the sun, and there wasn't a young man on the island but wished to marry her. But she showed no favour.

"Eventually it was a sailor-laddie from the mainland who won Maggie's heart. 'Frae then on,' the old woman said, 'her smile was for him alone.' She would wait and wish all week long for his coming, and when the boat came she would run down the bank and wait at the waterside for her lover. They would walk together along the shore until the sun was down and sometimes he would make drawings of her. At night in bed Maggie would tell her sister of her great love, and sigh for the day when she should be married.

"At that point the hag jabbed a finger at the picture and said in a shaky voice: 'Such eyes were made for weeping. Such a tender heart was made for sorrow.'

"The young man went away on a long voyage. Maggie implored her father to let them be married before he went, but he would hear nothing of it. Time enough to think of that, he said, when the voyage was over. It would prove whether her lover was true or no.

"Maggie said no more, but she cried all night on her sister's shoulder. She became pale and dull, and was like a cloud about the house. One night the old woman's mother found Maggie distracted with grief. She said she was no more than a shameless wench, and not fit to share a bed with a pure, innocent lassie. Her sister managed at last to soothe her to sleep.

"But the next morning Maggie was gone, and that same evening they recovered her body from the sea and brought her to the house."

Joan and Edgar had now circled the cottage and were heading back the way they had come. The barking of a dog died away behind them, leaving a double weight of silence, into which Edgar's voice broke again with a suggestion of effort.

"As if the loss of Maggie wasn't trouble enough for the family, all the inhabitants were against allowing her burial in the kirkyard. Maggie's father never recovered from the humiliation, and died soon after.

"I can see that old woman now, sitting there with her eyes fixed in a watery stare. Her little red pointed tongue kept flickering out over her shapeless lips. She seemed to have forgotten us.

" 'Poor Maggie was buried in the heather abune the bay, where she used to bide for her laddie,' she said, in a thin unsteady voice. 'But she waited long in her cauld bed, and nae lover came. Every Sabbath e'en my mother used to walk that way an' say a bit prayer for her sister buried there on the lonely moor. She feared the lass couldnae rest in unhallowed ground.'

"She turned up her eyes to the rafters, and her lips formed soundless words. Neither she nor her son stirred as we got up and went out into the night.

"The full impact of it didn't strike me till we got outside. In that small, smoky cottage, the youth of the old woman's mother had seemed a thing of yesterday. You could almost hear the echoes of the loud voice of Maggie's father forbidding her marriage, and the whispers of the two girls as they lay together in the darkness—perhaps in that very bed I saw.

"But as we walked back to the camp, the thought which had lain somewhere deep down in my mind—kept down by the sense of timelessness that prevailed in the place—suddenly asserted its shocking logic.

"That old woman was ninety years old if she was a day, and

the tragedy of Maggie had taken place before she was born—before her mother was married. What we were asked to believe eventually—what we were forced to believe eventually—was that the girl's body had been lying there a hundred years or more."

"But honey," Joan said to him—there could be no doubt of his seriousness, "that's not possible."

Edgar turned upon her. "Oh, but it is. The CO followed the matter up, and apparently it's been known before. Bodies have been preserved in the peat indefinitely, and that one might have lain there another century, if the tremors caused by our guns had not coincided with that long spell of rain and brought it to the surface."

"And that, I suppose," said Joan, not without relief, "is the end of the story?"

"It ought to have been. I think that in time Mac would have shaken off his obsession, or at least have kept it under until he left the island. It was obvious to everyone that he was mentally and morally ill. I had the thing out with him once.

" 'Do you really believe the body has been lying there all these years, preserved in the peat,' I asked him. 'If you insist on reducing it to a mere matter of chemistry, yes,' he said.

" 'And the alternative?' I prompted him. He flashed me a look of acute misery and repeated the old woman's words. 'She waited lang in her cauld bed, but nae lover came.'

" 'So?' I said.

" 'So there she must lie until her lover returns.'

" 'What nonsense,' I said, unable to suppress my skepticism. McCleod looked shocked and hurt, and walked away. That just about ended our intimacy.

"As I said, I think he would have recovered in time if—But about two weeks later it was reported that the hand had appeared once more, rising out of the heather as if it grew there.

"The CO began negotiations with the natives to have the body transferred to the kirkyard, but they wouldn't hear of it. They were as bitterly opposed to the idea as their grandfathers had been, and in the end the Major had to admit defeat. He had the body exhumed and buried deeper.

"But in less than a month it broke surface again, and men far less fanciful than McCleod began to express unorthodox opinions. Mac haunted the spot continually. He no longer confided in me, but I watched him pretty closely, and I could see that he was at breaking point.

"I saw the terror in his eyes when it was announced that half a ton of concrete was to be dumped over the burial place next morning.

"But I think it was the prank played by some of the less discerning of our messmates that broke McCleod. The boredom and the continuous foul weather tended to distort their sense of humour. For sanity's sake they had to get a laugh out of the affair, and Mac, with his mystical obsession, was the obvious butt. A deep grave had been dug, and the body wrapped in a blanket, left in an empty hut, in readiness for the morning.

"You may well imagine that the girl furnished just about the only topic of conversation that evening. It played on all our nerves a little, and most of us drank more than we were accustomed to.

"Some of the fellows grew indignant and pretty loud about the attitude of the islanders, and when they got up and went out I was fully convinced they were going to make trouble.

"Well, they were, but it wasn't the sort of trouble I expected. About a quarter of an hour later they staggered back into the mess with something wrapped in a blanket. There was a stunned silence, and one of them said in a tipsy voice: 'I say, you guys, we've brought the lady in for a drink. Show her we're gen'lemen, not like them other hypocrites.' "

Eyes wide with horror, Joan drew away with a cry.

"How horrible. Oh, Edgar, how could you!"

"Steady old girl. I assure you I had nothing to do with it. Of course it may not have been the body at all. I doubt if it was. After all they weren't so very drunk, and they were a decent crowd really."

"Didn't you ever find out then?" she asked. She fancied that there was a barely perceptible hesitation before he said: "No, I never found out."

"Then what happened?"

"Well, Mac had been sitting in a corner alone. His hair was all over the place and his eyes had a fixed, glassy look. He looked pretty far gone. When the boys barged in with—with the thing—the blanket, he just about went mad. It took six of us to hold him while we bundled those fools out of the door.

"That broke the evening up, and when the uproar died down—and there was an infernal row, I can tell you—we all went to our beds.

"The next morning McCleod was missing. We never saw him again. There was a large-scale search, and an exhaustive inquiry, both of which yielded nothing."

They walked in silence till they came once more to the tiny pool. Joan was searching in her mind for a possible explanation of it all, and a possible end. As they paused by the glistening water she said: "What do you think happened to him?"

Edgar said in a voice slightly hushed: "Well, it did occur to me that the party searching the island for McCleod, and the other mixing concrete and dumping it here, may possibly—just possibly—have been working at cross purposes."

"How dreadful," she said, as his meaning came to her. "And yet—" she took a pace nearer, casting a shadow across the pool, "—and yet how right."

"If the concrete hadn't sunk and become water-logged, we might perhaps still see the cross I marked on it before it hardened, and the letters RIP, which in this instance seemed to have more than their usual significance. It was—"

He was interrupted by the distant hoot of the boat's siren. Remembering the skipper's implied threat, they both glanced incredulously at their watches.

"It can't be as late as that!"

"I told you time had its own rules on Dunkelvie."

They joined hands and ran for it. The flowers Joan had carried in her hand during their long walk scattered slowly over the surface of the pool where she dropped them; and the pool looked serene and beautiful in the sun, though there was none to see.

The Ghost Hunter

Collected by Fr. Maurice Metayer

A young boy lived alone with his grandmother. As he grew older he became obsessed with a fear of ghosts. Such was his distress that he could not sleep at nights.

Repeatedly his grandmother told him, "Go to sleep like everyone else. There is no point in worrying, anyway; if you ever see a ghost you can be certain that it will quickly overpower you."

The boy, being stubborn by nature, would invariably reply, "No, no ghost would ever do that to me!"

When he became a young man, the boy decided to build himself an igloo. However he chose to place his home in an area somewhat apart from the other igloos so that he would be able to see anything that might approach from any direction.

His igloo was built like a large fort. Windows were cut out all around the sides and openings were made from which arrows could be shot at any evil spirits that might appear.

Once the igloo was completed the young man took up a nightly watch from within his fortress. Equipped with the bow and arrows given to him by his grandmother, he waited for the ghosts to appear. His grandmother and some of the other older people tried to persuade the young man to go to bed at night. They were afraid of what might happen to him if a ghost did appear.

"You will be killed!" they warned.

Obstinately the young man would reply, "No, no, nothing can happen to me." He was wrong to ignore the wisdom of his elders but obsessed as he was with his ideas, no one could change his mind.

Late one night, while maintaining his usual vigil, he thought he saw something move outside his window. He watched carefully, hoping that at last he might see a ghost. He strained to see what it could be. To his surprise it was not a ghost, but a beautiful young woman dressed in fine furs. She was standing near his grandmother's dwelling.

The young man was fascinated by her beauty and the more he watched the more smitten he became with her loveliness. He wanted her for his wife. Overcome with emotion, the young man forgot about everything else, including ghosts and spirits, bows and arrows. Without thinking any further and without even dressing in warm clothing, he dashed from his igloo and ran towards her.

Seeing the young man approach the woman spoke, "Come with me and you will be my husband. Let us go to my parents' home. Look over there and you can see the light from our igloo. It is the window of my father's house."

The young man looked and saw the illuminated window. After taking a few steps he hesitated, "No, I will not follow you. I am going to remain here."

The girl insisted, "But it is so near. Come, and we shall live together as husband and wife."

The girl's beauty and persistence finally overcame the boy's reluctance. He followed her through the night toward the bright light of her father's igloo.

For a long time they walked on together. Periodically the boy would turn around to view the receding lights of his settlement. It seemed as if they were getting farther and farther away from his home but the girl's home was no closer to them.

The boy was beginning to tire from the long journey. By now

leave that one alone. There are plenty of others." With that the two brothers went hunting elsewhere.

The young man was unable to dismiss the thought of the lone caribou from his mind. "Why does the old man not want us to go after that one?" he wondered. For some days thereafter the young man was haunted by thoughts of the caribou on the side of the mountain.

One day, while on another hunting trip, he made the decision to go after this caribou. The brothers-in-law tried to dissuade him but the young man became stubborn. He left his companions and set out on his own. He would kill the caribou, this caribou that was so mysteriously protected.

Approaching the mountain with caution, the hunter stalked his victim. He moved in as close as he could and then with deadly aim, let fly his arrow. The caribou fell. Immediately the young man started to skin the animal.

No sooner had the skinning commenced than a fog began to close in around him. Working quickly the hunter tried to finish his task before the fog completely blotted out the trail back to the settlement. When he had finished he left the caribou carcass on the ground, covered it with the stomach contents so that no animals would touch it, looked about him to be sure of his directions and set out for home.

Try as he might he could not find the right path. Each time he managed to proceed only a short distance before being confronted by a sharp cliff. He would then retrace his steps to the carcass, head himself in another direction and set out once more. The cliff rose from the fog to bar his path again and again. Moreover it seemed that the wall of rocks was closing in on him. He would be crushed!

Fortunately the young man always carried a charm of considerable magic with him. It was a piece of clothing with very short sleeves and was made from the skin of his ancestors. This garment was worn next to his body. Realizing the great danger he was in, the young man now called on the magic powers of his charm. He seized a sleeve and half removing the garment cried out to his ancestor, "Grandmother, I am in great danger!"

leave that one alone. There are plenty of others.'' With that the two brothers went hunting elsewhere.

The young man was unable to dismiss the thought of the lone caribou from his mind. ''Why does the old man not want us to go after that one?'' he wondered. For some days thereafter the young man was haunted by thoughts of the caribou on the side of the mountain.

One day, while on another hunting trip, he made the decision to go after this caribou. The brothers-in-law tried to dissuade him but the young man became stubborn. He left his companions and set out on his own. He would kill the caribou, this caribou that was so mysteriously protected.

Approaching the mountain with caution, the hunter stalked his victim. He moved in as close as he could and then with deadly aim, let fly his arrow. The caribou fell. Immediately the young man started to skin the animal.

No sooner had the skinning commenced than a fog began to close in around him. Working quickly the hunter tried to finish his task before the fog completely blotted out the trail back to the settlement. When he had finished he left the caribou carcass on the ground, covered it with the stomach contents so that no animals would touch it, looked about him to be sure of his directions and set out for home.

Try as he might he could not find the right path. Each time he managed to proceed only a short distance before being confronted by a sharp cliff. He would then retrace his steps to the carcass, head himself in another direction and set out once more. The cliff rose from the fog to bar his path again and again. Moreover it seemed that the wall of rocks was closing in on him. He would be crushed!

Fortunately the young man always carried a charm of considerable magic with him. It was a piece of clothing with very short sleeves and was made from the skin of his ancestors. This garment was worn next to his body. Realizing the great danger he was in, the young man now called on the magic powers of his charm. He seized a sleeve and half removing the garment cried out to his ancestor, ''Grandmother, I am in great danger!''

With this one call, the weather suddenly improved. The fog lifted and the stranded hunter was able to return home.

His in-laws had been worried about him. They wanted to know what had happened. At first the young man was reluctant to say anything. However his in-laws were insistent and after much persuasion he told them of the caribou, the fog and of his plea to his grandmother for help. But he did not tell them about the magic garment. The in-laws were not pleased. They forbade the young man from going on further hunting trips. He would have to remain at home while the brothers did the hunting.

For a long time the young hunter was left alone with little to do. He could only watch enviously while his brothers-in-law went in search of more game. As before, his feelings of jealousy finally got the better of him.

He spoke to his wife: "Your father has a kayak and a harpoon. I could make good use of these and follow the others when they go seal hunting."

His wife agreed to ask her father. "My husband wishes to hunt the seals. Could he borrow your kayak and harpoon?"

The father had no objections. "You may use them," he told the son-in-law. "My kayak is on the river bank and my harpoon is inside it. However before you go hunting there is something that you should know. You must only hunt the seals on this side of the island. Do not go to the other side. The seals on the far side are vicious. In your travels be sure to stay on the side closest to the land."

The three young hunters took the old man's advice and hunted the seals together, remembering not to go on the far side of the island. For many days they continued to hunt in this fashion.

Then one day it occurred to the husband that he should go to the other side of the island. He mentioned this idea to his brothers-in-law, but they would have none of it.

"No, we shall not go there; our father has forbidden it," they replied.

The young man was not so easily convinced. He would go by himself. Leaving his companions, he paddled toward the forbidden area. When he had reached the far side and was about to explore the shoreline, an extraordinary beast suddenly emerged from the depths of the sea and swam toward the hunter's kayak.

The young man threw his harpoon. The weapon found its mark and at the same instant the young man lost consciousness.

When he awoke he did not know where he was. He found himself on an ice field from which no land was visible. Looking around him the hunter spotted a huge snow house as large as a dance igloo. A man stood outside and motioned to him to enter.

The young man went inside. Around the igloo, standing in a circle, was a crowd of people. Lying on the floor was the monstrous seal that he had harpooned. The people pressed around him.

"You have killed our friend," they said. "Remove your harpoon from his body. When you have done so, cut yourself a large piece of meat. You will need this for food on the long journey that awaits you." The young man followed their instructions and made ready for a lengthy trip.

Dragging his kayak overland, the young hunter travelled throughout the long winter months. In time the kayak became worn to the point where it had to be dismantled. From the remaining pieces a package was made which the young man carried on his back.

By springtime this seemingly endless journey was far from over. With the arrival of the warmer weather other problems had to be faced. Pools of water were lying everywhere. Even when he reached land this problem remained. The island upon which the hunter was walking became covered with water. Moreover the depth of the water was increasing constantly. Recognizing that he was in extreme danger, the young man seized the sleeve of his magic garment and cried out, "Grandmother, I am in great danger!"

Immediately a great transformation took place. The young man was lifted into the air and was changed into a sea swallow. In bird-like fashion he was able to continue his journey, diving down over the water to snatch scorpion fish whenever he was hungry.

Eventually his flight took him to the area where he had lived with his grandmother long ago. Now everything was in ruins. All of the people were gone. His only hope was to return to his in-laws and so he used the magic power of the short-sleeved garment to transform himself back to a man.

Arriving at his in-laws' igloo the young man was confronted by his relatives. They were very curious about his strange disappearance and had many questions to ask. At first he refused to answer. He was ashamed to admit that he had gone to the far side of the island. But his in-laws would not leave him alone. In exasperation he finally gave in and decided to talk.

"All right! I am going to tell you everything, but first bring me a small bowl of water and place it at my feet."

Seated on the edge of the bed with the bowl of water before him on the floor, the young man proceeded to recount the entire story. No details were omitted save one. He did not mention his magic garment made from the skin of his ancestors. It was his last protection.

The young man completed his story by confessing that he had wanted to return to his grandmother's igloo, but that upon finding it deserted and in ruins, he had had no choice but to come back to the home of his in-laws.

His story angered the family but no sooner was the narrative completed than the young man, his magic garment in his hand, leaped from the bed and threw himself headfirst into the bowl of water. He disappeared and was gone forevermore.

Ghosts Have Warm Hands

Will R. Bird

By devious ways and both kinds of luck I finally reached Mount St. Eloi, and there to my astonishment and joy found Mel Baillie. He had gone down the line with mumps the same day I had, had also taken French leave from his hospital and was anxious to get with the boys. One of our lads, Gerald Gard, had been back of the lines with some ailment, had acquired mumps and given them to six different members of the 42nd.

We went over Vimy Ridge just at dusk. The Canadian attack of April 9 and 10 had left it a jungle of old wire and powdered brick, muddy burrows and remnants of trenches. The barrage had been the biggest of its kind to date. Much traffic was going along one main track, so we walked a way and sat in a crater to rest. I had walked at least ten miles and Baillie had done the same. Suddenly he spoke and pointed. To one side of us, in a sort of alcove to the crater, three dead men were reclining, gazing incuriously before them, their faces almost black. We rose at once and climbed from the place, and almost fell over another dead man crouched in a shell hole, rifle still in hand, as if ready to spring.

In the twilight just before darkness, we stood and looked

down over the Ridge on the enemy side. The first flares were rising in scattered places. We could not distinguish the lines. The air was damp and chilling, causing an unearthly feeling to predominate. The dead men, the solitary flares, the captured ground, gave us a sense of ghosts about, and hurried us over to a semblance of a trench leading down the slope.

Two hours later we found Fourteen Platoon, hardly recognizing it. The sergeant was there, and MacDonald, but most of the others were strangers. They were from the 73rd Royal Highlanders, a unit of the 4th Division so decimated during the attack on Vimy Ridge that they had been replaced by the 85th Nova Scotia Highlanders. MacDonald told us our company had gone straight through to the objective in spite of sleety snow and mud and confusion, but a flanking fire from the left, where the 4th Division had been held up, had taken a heavy toll. Belliveau and Jenkins and Joe McPherson had been killed in one area. One shell had wiped out Stevenson and two others. MacMillan had been shot in the stomach and had died after waiting hours in the trench. Gilroy and Westcott and Legge had been killed by machine-gun fire. Herman Black had run amuck. They found him almost at the bottom of the Ridge, near a battery position, with eight dead Germans about him, four of them killed by bayonet.

We hunted up Mickey and Ira Black and Eddie Cuvilier, Glenn Lunn and Tommy. They were sitting in the dugout after a hard day of rebuilding roads, each man suffering from bodily fatigue, crawling vermin and the clammy chill of mud-caked clothing, their faces brooding, enigmatic, even Mickey looking curiously old. Months before we had marched eagerly to Mount St. Eloi, our tin hats askew and with a cheeky retort for every comment, hiding whatever secret apprehensions we had. Now we had changed.

Two things I would remember about Vimy. The first was my experience in a working party. They sent Tommy and me one night to a place where they lowered us down, by a ladder that was quite vertical, to a chalk tunnel. It was cold outside, but when we got down there all sound stilled and it was warm. We had to shed our greatcoats and equipment at once. We tied sandbags over our boots and went, crouched on all fours, along a tunnel in solid chalk just four feet high and hardly three feet wide. At the face of it we worked in turns, and fast. The chalk face was sprayed with vinegar. Then one man cut it with a knife as it softened and passed back large chunks to his helper, who in turn placed them in the hands of another man near him. Thus the chalk removed was handed back and finally reached a small trolley drawn on tracks which took it to the hoist. There the stuff was raised and dumped, a sure sign to Fritz of underground operations. The air was dank and close and we sweated a great deal. It was amazing how far we proceeded in that one night. The man in charge forbade anyone speaking. At any moment it was possible the removal of a newly cut chunk might reveal a German dugout filled with men! For weeks afterwards my whole body would tense when I thought of that night.

The second episode I would remember was the issuing of whale oil to rub on our feet. It came in jugs and was colder than ice. It would prevent trench feet. Orders were that every man should rub it on his feet once in twenty-four hours while we were in those winter trenches. I did so religiously and never had the least trouble. But we had a big chap who had blustered much until we were within sound of the guns. Then he had tried in every way to get from the front, going on sick parade, complaining of blindness, even trying to wound himself slightly. He had been caught in the act and warned of what his punishment would be, so he never used the whale oil, although the sergeant who made the nightly check was told he did. The result was that after two days his feet started to swell. It was learned later he had purposely walked through wet places and the cold had penetrated. His feet became so bad he could not walk and finally he had to be taken out on a stretcher. The last we heard of him was from a lad who had been to see him in a hospital in England. Both feet were huge blobs of mis-shapen flesh. He could only move around on crutches and his feet would never be normal again.

We left the Ridge and went to Vimy village, relieving C.M.R.'s (Canadian Mounted Rifles) there, and doing working parties, digging trenches, putting up wire near the front line. During the first night I was sent out with two men as a covering party for the men working with the barbed wire. It was cold and miserable. We were made to inspect the area through binoculars so we would recognize the various landmarks and not put the wire in a wrong place. We were out soon after it was dark but did not take nearly enough wire the first time and had to return for more. So it was midnight before we were finished. Luckily the Hun did not hear anything, but it was very chilling to stay crouched in position for hours, and the night seemed endless. All I could think of was the fact I had no place to go when we were through. Getting our party ready had taken so long that I had had no chance to prepare any sort of shelter.

As we went back and drew near the railway embankment someone called in a low voice. I went over and found two of the men from the 73rd had dug a neat bivvy into the embankment. They were very decent chaps and insisted they had made the place wide enough to accommodate the three of us. We snuggled in, and with a ground sheet pegged to hold over our heads we were really comfortable. In seconds I was dead to the world.

The ground sheet pegged over our heads was pulled free and fell on my face, rousing me. Then a firm warm hand seized one of mine and pulled me up to a sitting position. It was very early, as first sunshine was glittering on the dew-wet grass. I was annoyed that I should have to do some chore after being out so late. I tried to pull free. But the grip held, and as I came to a sitting-up position my other hand was seized and I had a look at my visitor.

In an instant I was out of the bivvy, so surprised I could not speak. I was face to face with my brother, Steve, who had been killed in '15!

The first notice from the War Office had said: "Missing, believed dead." After a time one of his mates wrote to say a boot had been found with his name on it. The Germans had mined the Canadian trench and blown it up.

Steve grinned as he released my hands, then put his warm hand over my mouth as I started to shout my happiness. He pointed to the sleepers in the bivvy and to my rifle and equipment. "Get your gear," he said softly.

As I grabbed it he turned and started walking away rapidly. It was hard to keep up with him. We passed make-shift shelters filled with sleeping men of my platoon. No one was awake. Now and then a gun fired off toward the Somme or a machine-gun chattered, but on the whole it was a quiet morning. As soon as we were past the shelters I hurried to get close to Steve. "Why didn't you write Mother?" I asked.

He turned and the grin was still on his face. "Wait," he said. "Don't talk yet."

Then I noticed he had a soft cap on and no gas mask or equipment. Somehow he had learned where the 42nd was, and our "D" Company, but how in the world did he know where I was sleeping?

We left the company area and headed directly into a collection of ruins that had been Petit Vimy. "There's no one around here," I said. "How did you know where to find me?"

At that moment my equipment, slung hurriedly over one shoulder, slipped off and fell to the ground before I could catch it. As I stooped and retrieved it Steve went into a passageway in the ruins and I ran to catch him. Arrived there, I saw one way went right and the other left. Which way had he gone? "Steve!" I called. There was no answer, so I dropped my rifle and gear and ran to the right. It only took minutes—two or three—to get to the far side, but there was no sign of my brother. I ran back and called again, took the way to the left, searched and searched again, called repeatedly, but could not find him. Finally I sat down on my equipment and leaned back against a bit of wall. I was tired and sweating and excited. A great desire to find our officer and get the day off took hold of me, but I realized I did not know where the officer or sergeant-major were, and if I left the immediate area and Steve returned he would not know where I had gone. Probably he had no pass and did not want to be seen. If only I had not bothered with my equipment I could have kept up with him!

Minutes went by. I got up and made another search of the ruins. The sun began to glisten on the tops of the broken walls.

I settled back more comfortably on my equipment and heard the usual morning stir of guns firing registering shots. The sun got warmer. I dozed.

Suddenly I was shaken awake. Tommy had me by the arm and was yelling. "He's here! Bill's here!"

I stumbled up, dazed, looked at my watch. It was nine o'clock.

"What's made you come here?" Tommy was asking. "What happened?"

"What's all the row about?" I countered.

"You should know. They're digging around that bivvy you were in. All they've found is Jim's helmet and one of Bob's legs."

"Legs!" I echoed stupidly. "What do you mean?"

"Don't you know a big shell landed in that bivvy? They've been trying to find something of you."

It seemed utterly incredible. I put on my gear and followed Tommy. There was a great cavity in the embankment and debris was scattered over the whole area. Mickey came running to shake hands with me. Then the sergeant was calling and I saw he was talking with an officer.

When we got nearer I saw it was an artillery officer of high rank and saluted him.

"What made you leave the bivvy?" the sergeant asked. "The boys say you got in there with Jim and Bob."

"I did," I said. "I was there till daylight."

"What made you leave then?"

It was the artillery officer who asked the question, and I hesitated, felt it would sound foolish if I told them exactly what had happened.

"Don't be afraid," he said. "We're all friends."

He looked a real gentleman, so I told him my story in detail. He made notes in a book he carried, asking my name, where I was from, and all about Steve. Then he shook my hand. "You have had a wonderful experience," he said.

The sergeant looked as if he did not know whether to believe me or not, but a runner came with orders for another move and I hustled to get something to eat. Neither Tommy nor Mickey mentioned the matter to me through the day, and that night we were over to the left doing working parties again until late. I slept in a bivvy MacDonald and I had made but it was past midnight before I could doze off.

I had seen Steve as clearly as I saw Mickey. His warm hands had pulled me from the bivvy. His voice had been perfectly natural. He had the old half-grin I knew so well. He had saved my life.

I had joined the Methodist Church when I was fourteen and had been as decent as the average. At evenings in the Y.M.C.A. I loved the singing of hymns. I did not like the compulsory church service and the officers singing "O God, Our Help in Ages Past." But now I knew beyond all argument or theory, by any man learned or otherwise, that there was a hereafter, and there would never again be the slightest doubt in my mind about it.

For a few days I sensed that the sergeant had not believed my story but it did not worry me in the least. Then a batman let me know the officers had talked about the incident and regarded my story as the result of too much rum. This was rather amusing as I never took the ration and everyone in our company, except the officers who were new, was aware of the fact. However, in a few days the matter was forgotten by the men. And it was only as I lay ready for sleep that I thought of it.

The Mackenzie River Ghost

Julia M. Seton

About fifty years ago, some eminent scientists headed by Sir Oliver Lodge founded a Society of Psychical Research to ascertain if there was such a thing as a ghost in the ordinary sense of the word. They offered to investigate every supposed ghost and to do it in the calm cold way of exact science.

Hundreds of instances were sent them; and at least 99 per cent of the ghosts were totally dissipated under the disintegrating white light of the scientific approach. But a few there were that would not dissipate, that defied all attempts to explain them away. Among them was the ghost of the Mackenzie River.

In his early days—that is the eighties—Ernest Thompson Seton lived in the Northwest and knew many employees of the Hudson Bay Company. Among them was one bluff old Scotchman, Roderick MacFarlane. After many years, MacFarlane was retired, and lived in Winnipeg on a small pension. Each time Seton was in that city—about once a year—Mac and he would have a pleasant reunion over a good dinner.

About 1904, shortly after the Research Society had recorded a ghost that defied all ordinary explanation, they were dining together.

"Mac," Seton asked, "did you ever hear anything about the Mackenzie River ghost?"

"What ghost?" said he.

"A ghost that came in broad daylight to some men on the ice of the Mackenzie River. The story was told by a Hudson Bay Company Factor."

"Humph," said Mac, "that factor was me. But Lodge and his group didn't tell it right, nor at full length. I'll give you the facts right now if you like. You can do as you please with it after I'm gone. Do you want to hear it?"

"I sure do," said Seton. "Go on. Tell it as long as you please."

And this is the tale as MacFarlane told it that night:

Away back in the sixties, the Company thought there was a good chance of a successful trading post at the mouth of the Mackenzie, since this was Eskimo as well as Indian country and there was no post within 400 miles in any direction. So, with Sandy MacDonald for helper, I was outfitted for the job. When the summer came, we went to the Mackenzie Delta; and then, turning west, we selected the mouth of Peel River, where we built a couple of log houses, gathered a great pile of driftwood, and were ready for any fur trade that came along.

Next spring, when the river opened, we had a visitor by canoe—a young fellow named Middleton, about twenty-two years of age, a graduate of Oxford. He came equipped with letters from the High Council of our Company. He was filled with missionary zeal, his one hope and dream being to preach the Gospel to the Eskimos. He had no knowledge of the Eskimos or of their language; but he was undaunted by these difficulties, for he felt he was the chosen vessel to bring them the tidings of salvation.

He was the most impractical, helpless creature I ever saw in the wilds. He knew nothing but his Oxford and his Bible. He seemed to us sometimes like a madman. But he came with letters from the boss, so we had to take him into our family.

Yes, we received him first only on the strength of the letters; but after a month or two, we were ready to accept him on account of his personal worth and charm. Far from strong, and troubled with a hacking cough, he was nevertheless always ready to do his share, and more than his share, of the work. He was the one who got up first in the morning to light the fire and start the breakfast. He was the one to wash the dishes or scrub the dirty floor. It might be a zero blizzard outdoors, but he was the one who volunteered first to go out after more firewood.

He had brought a fiddle with him. He played well and had a string of good songs, and many a long, dreary winter night he whiled away for us, with his music and fun. I tell you we learned to love that poor fellow like a little brother.

But there was something sad in it all – that cough. It grew worse, and in spite of his bright spirits and cheerful soul, he was plainly fading away. Toward the end of the winter, he was so thin and weak that he couldn't go out of the door without getting frostbite. His cough was terrible, and he was spitting blood. Still he was bright, cheerful, and hopeful, and worked steadily at his Eskimo Grammar.

Then came days when he couldn't leave his bunk. One night he called us to him and said to me: "Mac, you know I'm not long for this world; I've felt my Saviour calling me home. You fellows have been so good to me I want to ask one last favor."

"There isn't anything in our power you can't ask," I said for both.

"When my soul goes on," he says, "I don't want my poor body to be thrust into a hole in the ground like some animal. Won't you please bury me in consecrated ground?"

"If it costs my last dollar and my life, I give you my word as a man that I will carry out your wishes," was my answer, and Sandy and I took his poor thin hands in ours, and we gave our solemn promise.

I tell you we were blubbering like two babies. But he wasn't; he was bright and happy.

A month later, the end came. He passed away, happy and peaceful.

The nearest consecrated burying ground was at Fort Resolution, 400 miles up the Mackenzie River and fully 500 from our post. We had no right to leave our post now, so we wrapped the corpse in caribou hides. Then with our axes we chopped a grave three feet deep in the ice that never melts on the Mackenzie Mouth.

When he was laid in it, we filled it level with water; and within a few hours, it was one solid mass of ice, level with the rest.

We put a little marker at each end of the place, which was all we could do at that time. I tell you living with that kind brave soul had done more for me than any book or sermon ever did. And Sandy and I just prayed for a way to carry out our promise.

Well, sir, it was full two years we had to wait, and we surely felt bad about it. But the chance came. The High Council of our Company sent orders to close up the post and travel at once with all books and records to Fort Resolution, where we were to report to the Superintendent of the District.

This gave us the chance we had looked for. We had two sleds, each with a team of fine big Husky dogs. On one sled we loaded the books and records of the post, our camping outfit, and grub for ourselves and dogs. On the other, we loaded the corpse which we were able to dig out after a couple of hours chopping. Sandy drove one team; an Indian who had been working for us drove the other. I, the boss, trotted ahead to break the trail.

I tell you it was a funeral like nothing else before – a double funeral. First, it was the end of Peel Post. You see, we knew there was no chance of rival traders by land; but we hadn't reckoned on the whalers, who came by sea and wintered not far away. They did some whaling, but their best trade was in fur with the Eskimos.

So we left a lot of valuable stuff in the cabins and nailed them up to keep off the bears. We knew no Eskimo or Indian would steal anything – they never do – and when the summer came, the boat brigade would salvage all.

But our big thought was the other sled. We must keep faith with the dead man. And away we went in easy stages to cover five hundred miles of ice and snow.

The Mackenzie River is two miles wide at the mouth. It has gravel banks and runs through a wide plain with only level snow till the black line of the forest begins, three to ten miles away on each side.

The best traveling for the sleds is up the middle of the ice, for there the wind has blown the snow away, and the ice is clear and firm for the runners.

So each morning we set out up the middle of the river ice, trotting along for maybe twenty miles. Then we made our noon halt. Driving to the nearest gravel bank, we hauled up onto the level plain. But there is no wood short of the pine forest miles away across the deep soft snow; so, in order to avoid this hard trip, we always carried on the front of one sled enough firewood to melt snow and boil it for our tea, and then a little more to cook our bacon.

After an hour's rest, we set out again for twenty miles more.

Then at night, we would leave the river, and break our way to the forest, where we made a comfortable camp with plenty of wood. And I tell you, I always kept the funeral sled by my bed, for I felt under a solemn vow to protect that. In the morning we gathered a new bundle of wood for the noon and set out again on the ice.

This was our daily routine for about a week. Then one day at noon, after we had driven up on the gravel bank ten feet above the river, I found we had lost some of our firewood. There wasn't enough to melt a kettle of snow and then cook our meal. So I said to the Indian: "Take the ax and chop through the river ice. If we can get to the water, that will save half the wood we need."

The Indian chopped and chopped till he was down the length of the ax handle. But still he was not through the ice. He called, and Sandy went down to see if there was any show of the water.

Soon he shouted back: "No good." I said: "Then look for an air-hole," and went down to help the search.

All of a sudden, we heard loud cries from a human voice on the river bank ten feet above us.

"Allez! Allez! Allez!" it shouted. Then *"Marchez! Marchez!"*

We did not suppose there was a human being within hundreds of miles of us. But again came the ringing *"Allez! Allez!*

Allez!"–the French that one always uses in ordering and driving the dogs harnessed before the sled.

In haste and amazement, we rushed up the bank and into view of our outfit. Here was the wide level expanse of snow bright in the winter sun, and *not a sign of a human being in sight except ourselves.* But there, lying in a groveling heap, were the ten big fierce Husky dogs, growling and rumbling, their eyes glowing, their hair bristling. The tracks showed plainly that taking advantage of our absence, the very first time they were left alone with the corpse, these hungry, half-tame wolves decided to attack and devour the body. But the moment they touched it, that ringing voice of command was heard driving them back in terror.

"Who spoke?" I asked almost in a whisper.

Sandy replied, also in a whisper: "Well, it was a white man's voice, for an Indian can't say *'Marche';* he says *'Mush.'* "

"Who spoke?" I said to the Indian. He pointed with emphasis to the corpse and added in a low tone: "His voice."

I tell you we never took any chances after that–night and day some one of us always was next the body. We felt under a vow to keep it safe and carry out our promise.

Day after day and night after night we went on with the same routine, some days making forty miles, but on many days of blizzard storm making little or nothing.

Finally we arrived at the upper reaches of the Mackenzie, where timber was plentiful, and where islands with trees were right in the river; so we had no trouble finding good campsites.

One evening we came on an island covered with timber, right handy, and decided to camp there. Its shores were clay cutbanks about ten feet high. We left our two sleds on the ice, but Sandy and I climbed up. The Indian caught the dogs one by one, and we hauled them up onto the level top. Here we turned them loose, for I knew they would not leave the fire, and that ten foot drop was as good as a fence all around.

About nine o'clock, I was smoking my pipe before turning in, when I heard a strange faraway call on the wooded shore.

"Ye-hoo-ooo-ooo!"

I started up, for it was repeated.

"Ye-hoo-ooo-ooo!"

At first I thought it was a horned owl, or maybe a wolf call. But again it came with human intonation.

"Ye-hoo-ooo-ooo!"

"Say, Sandy, there's some one out there, a lost traveler." So I went to the edge of the island, and shouted back.

"Hallo! Hallo, there! Who are you?" There was no answer, even to a second call, so I came back to the fire. Very soon again there came:

"Ye-hoo-ooo-ooo!"

I went to the edge of the timber, and shouted: "Who are you? Why don't you come on? Can't you see the fire?"

There was no answer to this, and I said to my pal:

"Say, Sandy, I don't feel comfortable about leaving our charge on the ice. The dogs can't get near it; but anyway, let's put it up a tree."

So we three went down in the darkness; and after much trouble, got our burden safe up a thick bushy tree. We heard no more calls in the night.

Next morning, as my helper was packing and making ready for a start, I prowled around in the snow and on the ice. There I learned from the tracks that all the previous evening, and maybe for a couple of days before, we had been followed by a wolverine. Our charge would have been unprotected by the dogs and exposed to the wolverine, which certainly would have found and disfigured it, had we not acted on the weird warning that came in time.

After that, our journey continued with little incident till near Christmas, when we reached Fort Resolution.

There I turned over my charge to the Archbishop, who laid it by the altar in the church, promising to attend to all proper ceremonies as soon as feasible—which meant as soon as the springtime made it possible to dig a grave.

That night we three travelers slept in the rampasture, which is the name of the bunk-house in a Hudson Bay Fort.

The moon was full, shining on the snow, and, through the window, lighted up the place well. About ten o'clock I was awakened with a sudden feeling of alertness. I sat up as unsleepy as could be, and there right opposite to me were Sandy and the Indian both sitting up.

Then there came on me an overwhelming feeling of bliss, of happiness complete; and in the gloom, I thought I saw on Sandy's face the same expression of rapture. I do not know any word to describe the sensation but "ecstasy." It gradually faded away. We gazed at each other and at the door and at nowhere.

I said: "Sandy, did you see anything?"

"No," he whispered.

"Did you?" I asked the Indian.

He shook his head.

"Did you feel anything, Sandy?"

"I did," he said. "I was filled with joy."

"What was it?" I asked.

In a low but certain voice, he said: "He came in gratitude to us for carrying out our promise. Thank God we didn't fail him! We have surely had our reward."

Kismet

Johann Polberg

The people of the West Coast talked about the hot, dry summer of 1970 for years, but to Frank and Mary Holmes the memory of it held a special poignancy. Day after day the sun had shone down from a cloudless blue sky. Long before noon the freshness of the morning would turn to cloying heat. In the city people kept in the shade of the skyscrapers; businessmen shed their jackets and at the end of the day came home exhausted. City road crews, stripped to the waist, were burned brown by the sun as they worked filling in the previous winter's potholes. Anyone with free time went to the beaches or the parks.

In the suburban shopping centres the heat shimmered over the black-topped parking lots. The air-conditioned shops were like oases in a desert. Mary only went out once a week to the bank and stores, and then as early in the morning as possible, before returning gratefully to her tree-shaded home high on the hillside of North Vancouver.

Now that she and Frank were alone, Mary had taken up painting again, putting in long hours in the empty room that had become her studio. She worked every day completing pieces for a show planned by a local gallery for October. While the boys were growing up she had filled sketch book after sketch book with pencil, pastel, and water colours. Using these notes as a basis for her compositions, she worked on big canvases now, learning to handle acrylics as well as oils, frustrated and exhilarated at the same time.

But she was tired. Somehow the tiredness was always there, and the heat made it worse. Occasionally, she sat in front of a half-finished canvas too exhausted to go on. Mary and Frank spent a month at Comox, where Mary sat in the shade, reading and watching their grandchildren play. Later, when she looked at the snapshots taken with the children, she was shocked at how worn out she appeared.

"Frank, being fifty shouldn't make me look like that," she said. "I look like a ghost."

"Then go see Doc Watson. Get him to check you over and see why you're always so tired. I can't have you sick, not now, when we finally have time to do some of the things we've put off for so long."

So the appointment was made, and one stifling hot afternoon Mary waited her turn in the doctor's office. Jack Watson had been their doctor for years, and a friend, too, a source of comfort to Mary and Frank when their boys were growing up.

"Your turn next, Mrs. Holmes." The nurse stood at the doorway to the inner offices. When Mary rose from her chair the floor seemed to tilt and she lost her balance briefly. But she recovered without falling. "This heat really gets to me," she said to the nurse. "I'll be glad when it rains." The nurse took Mary's arm and walked with her to the examining room.

"I don't hurt," she told the doctor. "I don't feel ill, but I'm tired. Everything is such an effort. I feel like a clock that is running down." Her voice was apologetic.

After the examination Mary asked, "What have you found, my dear Watson?" The doctor sat quietly, looking solid and reliable. His thick brown hair was white now, but his face looked youthful and his eyes bright.

He smiled. "I don't quite know yet. I want you to see a specialist, a heart specialist. Dr. Orton."

"Good heavens, a heart specialist. That sounds a bit scary."

"Not necessarily. We have to get you going again. Orton may have the solution." Dr. Watson wrote something on a card and then handed it to Mary. "He's in the Medical Building on Fourteenth Street."

The windows had been left down, but the car in the parking lot was insufferably hot. Mary drove home carefully, beads of sweat on her forehead, her mind full of questions, even more tired than usual. She had never really been sick. She took care of herself. She did nothing to excess. Maybe she had been too intense about her painting? Perhaps she should give that a rest for a while? How would she tell Frank? Good grief, a heart doctor. What could she say?

In a few days, Mary saw Dr. Orton. There were more tests, x-rays, questions, probings. The heat continued. The sun glared down on parched lawns and drooping flowers. The neighbourhood children quarrelled. The mothers scolded. Mary lay quietly on a lounge chair under the trees in the garden, tired, tired, tired.

The day before the second appointment with Dr. Orton, Frank came home to find her too tired to sit up. He picked up her limp, frail body and carried her to the car. In the hospital nurses, doctors, and technicians went quickly and efficiently to work. Mary was put to bed. A girl in a white coat came with a tray of vials and took blood. A nurse with a stethoscope checked her heart regularly. The pharmacist came with a capsule for her to swallow. Dr. Orton gave her an injection.

Mary watched them all listlessly. Somehow it seemed to be happening to someone else. At last, when someone brought her a tray with supper, she roused herself to say, "Thank you. I feel better now. It's this awful heat. I wish it would rain."

"It's much more than the heat." Dr. Orton's face was grave. "You have an aneurysm, and we must do something about it quickly. You need an operation. But we need some more tests first."

Hospital routine took over their lives. Frank came daily, sometimes twice a day. They talked of the simple, familiar things they shared and loved. Dr. Watson came every morning and often in the evening, always quietly optimistic. Little by little he explained to Mary the operation that was to come. There were more tests, painful and exhausting.

The head nurse looked in on Mary one day and said, "You're lucky. You have the best surgeon around here and the best doctor, too. He really cares about you. I'm sure you will be okay."

The heat continued. Every day seemed the same. Finally Mary was wheeled into surgery. Frank looked gaunt and weary that day. At home everything had seemed unnaturally quiet to him. Then he realized that he had forgotten to wind the grandfather clock. It was as though a life had gone out of the house, he thought. He showered, found something to eat, and left for the hospital.

Mary was in the Intensive Care Unit, very pale, very still, but awake. "I've been wired for sound," she whispered when Frank came in. "Look at all the gadgets."

"Five minutes, Mr. Holmes," said the nurse. Dr. Watson came in and stood beside Frank. "She'll be all right. Give her a few days and she'll perk right up."

Mary looked at him with a ghost of a smile. "Ah, my dear Watson . . ."

"Quiet, woman. Come on, Frank. Time's up."

On the fifth day Frank found Mary back in her room. Clouds finally feathered the sky. The air was muggy and oppressive. Time seemed to be suspended, waiting for something to happen. The over-worked staff were exhausted. The patients were fretful, and Mary lay listless in her high bed looking out at the mountains. The snow was gone now, even from the peaks, the ski runs bare, ugly gashes on the hillsides.

The wind rose and the water in the inlet looked grey and restless. Dust devils whirled at the street corners. Mary was allowed to sit up in a chair, to walk slowly to the window and look out over the city. She watched thunderheads rolling across the sky. "Let it rain," she prayed silently. "Let it rain."

Tired, she crept back to bed and slept. When she woke it was unnaturally dark. Suddenly thunder crashed overhead, lightning flashed, but there was still no rain. She heard footsteps in the corridor and her heart said, "Frank," even before he came through the doorway. How tired he looks, she thought.

He kissed her and sat quietly as she picked at the meal that was brought to her. He told her the boys had phoned, that the grandchildren all sent their love. When the tray was taken away she lay back on the pillows with a sigh. She was suddenly aware of the rain beating against the windows. The room grew darker.

She was so tired of being in bed. Sitting up, she swung her legs over the edge of the bed and stood up facing the door. It seemed lighter there, and she walked into the corridor, surprised to feel no pain, no fatigue. Her sense of well-being was beyond anything she had felt before.

The corridor ended just past her door, and the windows there looked out over the city to the Lions' Gate Bridge and the open sea. The last glow of sunset shimmered on the horizon. The sea was calm and opalescent. The storm had passed. There was peace. "How good it is to be cool," she thought, looking down at the rain-slick streets. A police car and an ambulance went by, lights flashing.

She heard hurried footsteps behind her, heard urgent voices, but she did not turn from the window. Then she realized that she was not alone. Dr. Watson had come up silently and stood behind her. He did not have on his white hospital coat. Instead, he wore slacks and a casual sweater.

"Well, my dear Watson, what are you doing here?"

He looked at her intently, unsmiling, and said, "Get back in bed . . . now."

The sharp urgency of his voice surprised her and she started to speak. "I want to see the last of the sunset, it . . ."

His voice was harsh and preemptory. "No. Get back in bed. Quickly."

Mary's eyes filled with tears as she turned back towards her room. She saw people around her bed: Dr. Orton, Frank, another man in a white coat, the two nurses. She closed her eyes and slid into darkness. Far away, she heard Dr. Orton's voice. "It's all right. She's coming out of it."

She opened her eyes and saw Frank's face bending over her. She felt his hands, warm and strong, holding hers.

"Mary, sweetheart." The intensity of his voice reminded her of the happy times when they made love. She felt suddenly peaceful, euphoric. She clung to his hands and smiled.

"Good girl," Dr. Orton said briskly. "You gave us a fright." He turned to the nurse. "She'll be all right now. Her pulse is steady and her colour is coming back."

Someone wheeled equipment out of the room. The nurse tidied the bed and brought an extra blanket. "It's cooler now, with the rain," she said. "You'll sleep well tonight."

In the morning Mary woke refreshed. The sun was shining, but the intense heat was over. The mountains stood clear against the sky, and a few white clouds drifted in the wind.

"Whatever happened last night?" Mary asked Dr. Orton when he came into her room. "I can't remember properly."

"You had a bad turn. Your heart stopped suddenly for a minute, but you're fine now. Not to worry." Dr. Orton put his stethoscope aside. "Everything is ticking along nicely. You'll be able to go home before long."

"Where is Dr. Watson this morning?"

"Away for a few days. He works too hard, takes his work too seriously." He turned and left the room.

In ten days Mary was home, marvelling at how well she felt. Frank had time off. It was almost like a holiday. She wandered through the garden, delighted to see the flowers refreshed and blooming again. She studied the half-finished canvas on its easel and thought how it would look when it was completed.

"I must phone Jack Watson. He was so kind to me when I was in the hospital," she said to Frank one afternoon as they had tea in the garden. "Except the night of the storm. He was as cross as a bear. He must have been worried about something."

Frank looked at her in puzzlement. "He wasn't there that night, Mary. We didn't tell you, but on the way to the hospital in the downpour, he skidded out of control on the bridge. The car was totalled; Jack died instantly."

Mary put her cup down carefully and leaned back in her

chair. She was very still and sat with her eyes closed. Frank rose and bent over her. "Mary, are you all right?" he asked gently.

"Oh, yes," she said. She opened her eyes and smiled. "He sent me back, Frank. Jack Watson sent me back to you."

Ghost Story

Christie Harris

Once there was a lively little prince who craved adventure. But it was not the kind of adventure you might expect of an Indian boy in the wild, mountainous Northwest. He did not crave seal hunting or goat hunting in the hills. He did not even yearn to go out catching eagles. He wanted to do something much, much more exciting. He wanted to go adventuring where his body could not take him.

One day he told his four friends about it.

The five little Eagle-crest nobles were watching an eagle soar high above them when the prince blurted it out. "I'm going to move through the air, too," he told them. "And see the faraway world the way an eagle sees it."

"But Sea-Hawk!" his friends protested. "Nobody can move through the air."

"No body," he agreed. "So that's why I've got to get out of my body."

His friends were not as astonished as you might think. In those days of long ago, people were very much aware of their two selves: their body self that would die, and their spirit self that would live on forever. They were very much aware of the two worlds they lived in: the solid world of everyday things and everyday people, and the gossamer world of ghosts.

"I'm going to journey through the air," Sea-Hawk went on. "And I'm going to journey through the ocean and see that world too, the way a whale sees it."

"But Sea-Hawk!" his friends protested.

Only a shaman, a medicine man, learned how to get out of his body to make such fantastic spirit journeys.

"I'm going to be a shaman," the prince confided to his friends.

"But—" his friends protested again, because everyone knew that Sea-Hawk's family intended him to be the head chief his birth entitled him to be.

"I'm going to be a shaman. And you're going to help me," he told his comrades.

The very next day, the five boys slipped away from the village. And they kept on slipping away, day after day after day. To keep people from guessing what they were up to, they always took their bows and arrows or their balls and hooked sticks or their spears and hoops.

When they reached their secret place in the woods, they cached their sports equipment and started playing shaman.

It took a long time to build a secure little hut to keep their things in and to mark it with their identifying crests. It took a long time to make a crown of bird claws and a dancing apron that clattered with hazelnut shells. It took a long, long time to make four sets of regalia for the shaman's helpers, five medicine rattles, and decorated boards with sticks for beating time, and bone whistles. And it took an even longer time to create medicine songs and dances. But it was such fun that they all decided to become shamans, with Sea-Hawk the most important shaman, of course. And they talked endlessly about the adventures they would have, high in the air, deep in the ocean, and even over the misty bridge into the shivery Land of Ghosts.

The days flew by, and the moons, and the seasons. The years seemed to have wings. The boys grew older and bigger. Yet their ambition never changed. They were still going to be shamans.

Since their families did not know about the secret games, the five Eagles were trained and educated like other youths of their class. Nobles were expected to be stronger and more skillful and more graceful than common people. So they swam in the icy water every morning and then had their bodies whacked and rubbed with green boughs until their skin flamed like the sunrise. They learned to paddle and hunt and fish, to speak eloquently, and to perform the tribal ceremonies. They learned the art and the law, their own rights and their neighbors'.

Actually, they were glad of their training, for they knew that medicine men needed tough bodies, alert senses, and very sharp minds, as well as superb artistry in performance. They paid rapt attention to the storytellers and the singers and the dancers, especially when the performer was a professional doctor.

Yet they always found time for their secret rites in the woods. In fact, they were still so wrapped up in the old boyhood dream that it came as a shock when the chiefs began making arrangements for Sea-Hawk to take his destined place in society.

Suddenly, his relatives were readying the envoys who would go out to the distant villages, delivering the invitations to the potlatch, to the great feast at which Sea-Hawk would be installed in his proper place in the tribe. Suddenly, people were talking about the great name that would be his rightful hereditary title. They were talking about the famous crests that would be presented to him with the accompanying songs and stories and dances. Suddenly, there was no more time for dreaming wild dreams about fantastic spirit journeys.

Aghast at the fact that his family's plans for him were already in motion, Sea-Hawk fled to the hideout in the woods, with his friends close behind him.

"It's now or never," he gasped. "I'll have to tell them. But what if they won't let me be a shaman?"

"Oh," his best friend countered, though none too confidently, "they'll let you be a shaman if you show them you have enough talent to be a good one." For everyone knew that shamans–

those men and women in touch with the other world—were greatly respected in the villages. Sometimes they were even more honored than the head chief. Always they were more feared, more deferred to.

"Well," Sea-Hawk agreed, also none too confidently, "then maybe I'd better show them I have talent, IF I do have talent."

He meant a talent for touching the other world, for communicating with the ghosts and spirits who could do so much good or so much harm to people. Who could make them sick or well.

"There's only one way to find out," Sea-Hawk went on.

"And there's no time to lose," his best friend, Little Wolf, reminded him.

"There's no time to lose," Sea-Hawk agreed.

"It had better be impressive," Little Wolf urged.

"Yes, it had better be impressive," Sea-Hawk agreed, knowing that there was only one way to impress his family with his talent for touching the other world. And it was no way for a coward. With so little time to convince them of a true gift for medicine, he would have to touch the cold, clammy world of ghosts. And the only way into that world was through the graveyard.

"It's now or never," he said. And turning about, he darted off toward the burial ground, with his four friends close behind him.

The burial place was set well in back of the village, on the bank of a brook that flowed dark and silent through yielding moss and muskeg. To reach it, the boys had to skirt the village and then follow a trail that twisted through dark, drooping cedars and past firs that stood silent in the silence of a world hushed by deep, deep, green mosses. Pale owls flitted like ghosts among the trees; and like ghosts they made no sound in passing.

Newly alert to the dark brooding of the forest, the boys were almost as silent in their passing. And newly aware of the hovering presence of the ghosts of the dead, they emerged quietly into the openness of the graveyard.

Dusk was falling. The shadows of the trees were creeping

out silently to shroud the grotesquely shaped and grotesquely fruited grave trees. For, slung up in the trees, were the painted coffins of the dead; and where ancient coffins had broken open, there was the glimmer of scattered bones under the trees. There were old, old skulls, green with moss and haunted with dark, empty eye sockets.

Unnerved by what he must do, Sea-Hawk slipped quickly toward the mortuary poles of the great chiefs. In the fading light, the carved Ravens and Bears and Eagles and Wolves and Killer Whales on the poles seemed to be waiting. He looked up at the great carved cedar plank that hid the totem-painted coffin of his dear old grandfather.

"You have the emblems of our family set like a fort around you," he whispered to his grandfather. "Our supernatural helpers will help me, too." There was power in the great totems. He could feel the power pulsing out into the silence of the graveyard.

Then he saw a new, empty Eagle coffin resting on a broad, low pole. He saw a white owl glide over it, silent as a disembodied spirit. He moved swiftly toward it, then turned to look at his four friends.

They swallowed their protests. Sea-Hawk must prove his talent for touching the cold, clammy world of ghosts.

Only a light mist wreathing through the grave trees and mortuary poles suggested the Land of Ghosts that lay just beyond them. Only a heavier drift of mist above the dark brook suggested the ghost bridge that spanned an invisible ghost river, giving the ghosts of the dead their way out of the Land of Ghosts into the graveyard where they still kept watch over the skeletons they had once used.

The sudden, eerie screech of an owl curdled the boys' blood.

Sea-Hawk swallowed. Then he laid a resolute hand on the empty coffin.

"But Sea-Hawk!" His friends could not help voicing one protest.

"The emblems of my family are set like a fort around me," he answered. And climbing into the coffin, he lay down. He lay utterly still and silent. Still and silent as death.

His four friends, really frightened now, looked at one another.

"We'll stay," Little Wolf announced. "Who knows what will happen?"

The others nodded in solemn agreement. They stood hushed with awe. For there were great forces surging silently in the world all about them. And with their fear-sharpened senses, they were more deeply aware of those forces than they had ever been before.

The world darkened. And nothing moved. Nothing but the eerie owls who glided over the graveyard, pale and silent as ghosts.

One lighted on the coffin and stared at them with large, round, yellow eyes fixed immovably in their sockets.

"I think I'd better go home," one of the boys whispered. "He's well off the ground. So the animals won't get at him." And he slipped away, along the trail to the village.

Little Wolf moved stealthily to look into the coffin. He caught his breath. "He's dead," he whispered. Then he leaned closer. "No, his heart's beating," he reported. "But that's all," he said. And his eyes were wide with wonder. "Do you think his soul has already left his body?"

"I think maybe I'd better go home too," one of the other boys said. "What could we do if something did happen?" And he slipped away, along the trail to the village.

A little later, the third friend slipped away.

Only Little Wolf was left in the graveyard with the still, silent, empty husk of his best friend.

Where was Sea-Hawk? he wondered. Moving through the air, seeing the world as an eagle saw it? Or moving deep through the ocean, seeing that mysterious world as a whale saw it?

The moon rose, touching the grave trees and mortuary poles with ghostly silver and making the dark shadows darker than they were. A faint breeze stirred. And there were tiny, cautious rustlings.

Suddenly, Little Wolf shivered. He felt his hair rise on his neck. He felt his skin tighten and turn cold at the base of his spine. The ghosts had come over the bridge. The ghosts were moving into the graveyard.

An owl shrieked. And Little Wolf fled along the shadowy trail that twisted through dark, drooping cedars, past firs that stood silent in the silence of a world hushed by deep, deep, green mosses.

He burst into the house, darted toward the cheerful light of the fire, and felt a hand on his shoulder.

"Where is Sea-Hawk?" one of the prince's uncles demanded.

Little Wolf swallowed. Where *was* Sea-Hawk? He licked his dry lips. "He's . . . lying in a coffin in the burial ground."

The hand tightened on his shoulder. "Tell the chief!"

The boy moved reluctantly toward the waiting figure of the chief. And looking into those intent, observant eyes, he could tell nothing less than the whole truth.

"Great Tribe!" the chief said, turning toward the silent, waiting people, "We are going to the burial place to bring the prince home. Light your torches!"

The order raced from house to house in the village. And soon the tribe was moving in single file along the trail, their torches of pitchwood and maple bark and oolachan fish throwing fantastic shadows on the drooping cedars and on the firs that stood silent in a world hushed by deep, deep, green mosses.

In the burial ground, the torches made rings of flame to light the still, silent body of the prince, while men lifted it out of the coffin and laid it on a cedar plank covered with fresh mats. Then a low chant started as the flames moved slowly along the forest trail again, back toward the waiting village.

The shamans circled the prince with wild, frenzied dances before the men laid him close to the fire in the chief's house. And the stirring flames seemed to continue the spirit-dancing as they flickered over the watching faces of the people and reached into the gloomy corners to reveal the startling faces carved on the great cedar houseposts. Supernatural Eagles and Bears, too, seemed to be breathlessly waiting, to see what was going to happen to the prince who had dared the cold, clammy ghosts in the graveyard.

He had dared the ghosts without proper training in handling

the wild, surging, invisible forces of the world. And now he seemed dead.

Yet his heart was beating faintly. His body self was still waiting for the return of his spirit self. But was that self lost? Was it unable to find its way back to its body? Would it stay lost until the heart stopped?

The people watched and wondered, their eyes on the frantic shamans. But the prince did not stir.

While it was still night, messengers slipped away to other villages to summon other shamans. They carried the chief's offer of a rich reward to the medicine man who could bring the prince's spirit self back to his body.

Excited by this challenge, all the shamans came at once. And for four days and four nights, they worked over the boy in turn. They crowned their long straggly hair with circles of grizzly-bear claws, and round their gaunt bodies they tied dancing aprons that clattered with puffin-bill fringes. They beat their medicine boards with wild rhythms and shook their medicine rattles. Framed against the gloom of the great cedar house by the red glow of the flames, they leaped and danced themselves into frenzies to activate deep, occult powers in themselves. Sometimes one would fall into a trance and lie as though dead while his spirit self went searching for the prince's. And one by one, they laid their most powerful carved bone charms on the youth's body.

They were all beating their boards near him when the prince opened his eyes.

At long last, his spirit self had come back to his body. And the wild joy of the tribe rang through the house, through the village. People laughed and wept and chanted as the shamans were rewarded for their great work.

For some time, the prince lay by the fire, still but alert, as though exhausted yet stimulated by some fantastic adventure. His four friends stood watch.

"Where were you?" they demanded.

"What happened?"

"Were you frightened?"

"Did you really move through the air?"

"Did you really see the world as an eagle sees it?"

"Did you see any ghosts?"

"What did you see, Sea-Hawk?"

"I saw . . ." The prince's eyes seemed to hold the almost-frightening brightness the boys had often glimpsed in medicine men's eyes. "I saw the spirit self of every man shimmering around his edges . . . men . . . trees . . . animals . . . flowers. . . . Every living thing was edged with a misty glow."

"Even . . . us?" Little Wolf asked in an awed whisper.

"Even you, Little Wolf." Suddenly Sea-Hawk sat up and laughed at his friend's wide-eyed wonder. "Your spirit self has a very strong glow. And some day you'll make a spirit journey with me. Some day you'll see . . . what . . . I saw." His voice sank into an awed whisper. His eyes went wide with wonder. "There's nothing in our world like it, Little Wolf," he said. "I am going to be a shaman."

"If they let you," Little Wolf cautioned. For all through the dreadful days he had sensed that the chief still planned to have Sea-Hawk installed in his rightful, hereditary place in the tribe. It was what everyone had always expected. Changes were not easy in the tribal hierarchy. A noble's duty could not be simply tossed off.

Sea-Hawk was not listening. Caught up in what he had seen on his fantastic spirit journey, he fingered the carved bone charms the shamans had piled on his body, then he hung them around his neck. And finally, as though the power in the charms was surging into him, he leaped up. He lifted his head fiercely. And his eyes blazed. "I will be a very great shaman," he predicted.

Little Wolf caught his breath. Then he shook his head to clear it. He blinked his eyes, twice. For he had glimpsed something. For one moment it had been as if Sea-Hawk were standing against the Northern Lights. But he must have been mistaken, he told himself. It must have been the firelight. Little Wolf shook his head again.

The chief was Sea-Hawk's uncle. And the chief's plans for his heir seemed to be going ahead exactly as before.

Then grief struck the village. Suddenly, without warning,

the chant of sorrow swelled out from the second largest house in the village, the house with the Wolf totems. "AIE AIE AIE! He has left us! AIE AIE AIE!" Over and over it swelled. "AIE AIE AIE! He has left us!"

Sea-Hawk raced into Wolf House, with his friends close behind him. For it was the home of his father's Wolf clan family.

His father's sad eyes lighted at the sight of his son. "It is the old chief," he said.

"AIE AIE AIE! He has left us! AIE AIE AIE!"

"He had so wanted to see if you would manage to become a shaman," Sea-Hawk's father confided.

"He will not only see," the youth told his father. "He will join in the ceremonies. I will restore him to life."

"My son!" The father's eyes were intent on his son. "Can you do that?"

"I can do that."

Sea-Hawk fled to the secret place in the woods, with his friends in attendance.

"Our regalia is ready," he remarked, taking a crown of grizzly-bear claws out of a carved chest.

"For what?" Little Wolf asked.

"Yes. Ready for what?" the other friends demanded, as they lifted out the sacred charcoal and eagle down, the medicine rattle and the clattering dancing apron and the white tail of an eagle. Sea-Hawk couldn't really be about to do what he had promised.

Again, as Sea-Hawk looked at his friends, his eyes seemed to hold a wild, unearthly brightness. "I am going to bring the old chief back to life," he announced with quiet conviction.

There was no interfering with the prince's plans. He knew what he was going to do, and how he was going to do it. All he wanted from his friends was a spirited performance as shaman's helpers. "Don't worry about it!" he told them, "I'm not counting just on you. I have a supernatural helper now."

"You have a . . . ?" Little Wolf looked in amazement. Only a very great shaman had his own supernatural helper. The owl? he wondered. The owl that had lighted on the coffin and stared at them with its large, round, yellow eyes fixed immovably in their sockets. He would know for sure as soon as Sea-Hawk started dancing, because the owl, if it was the owl, would possess the prince's body and use it in owl ways. The prince would glide silently, and swoop as an owl swooped. He would shriek the blood-curdling owl's shriek. He would no longer be just Sea-Hawk.

Since the performance was to be in Wolf House where the dead man lay, the Eagle chief was not involved. In fact, he knew nothing about it until it had started, until all the villagers were slipping into the sorrowing house, their eyes wide with excitement.

The house hushed itself as the prince and his four attendants entered. It was the youngest medicine party the tribe had ever seen.

The prince looked superbly confident, his proud features blackened with charcoal. Sacred white eagle down floated away from his shaman's crown of grizzly-bear claws as he moved, and the puffin-bill fringe on his dancing apron clattered softly in the silence of the great gloomy cedar house. A medicine rattle shook lightly in his right hand, while the white eagle tail in his left hand made graceful sweeps through the air. And the light in his eyes leaped like the fire that blazed in the center of the house.

People caught their breath. Perhaps the prince could bring the old chief back to life. They hugged their blankets close and kept their gaze on his every movement. They swayed with him, and echoed his every owl hoot.

It was evening. Sparks leaped up toward the smoke hole, and out toward the dark sky as the shaman prince began to sing a strange song, a song filled with soft hoots and sudden screeches. Then he began to dance in a way that not even his close friends had ever seen him dance before. Each time he circled the fire he seemed to swoop silently down on the dead man. And whenever he held still, as if searching about him for direction, he swiveled his whole head as though his eyes had been fixed immovably in their sockets. And after his fourth circling of the fire, his swoop toward the dead man was accompanied by a blood-curdling shriek.

"It *is* the owl." Little Wolf's lips made the words, but his voice did not rise to say them.

When the shaman prince finally spoke, however, it was in his own voice. "The old chief is now in the village of the Ghosts," he said. "And my supernatural helper says that I shall bring his soul back to his body. . . . Fetch me a fragrant new cedar-bark blanket!" he commanded.

His four attendants glided away as if they too were possessed by owl spirits. And they handed him the wrap in silence.

Sea-Hawk exchanged his white eagle tail for the cloak. Then, speaking in a loud, carrying voice, he commanded everyone to stay in Wolf House until he came back. They were to join his attendants, he said, in beating on the hollow cedar planks and on the skin drums. "And sing as loud as you can to coax the soul back!" he ordered.

He slipped out into the darkness of the night alone. Silent as an owl, he followed the trail that twisted through the dark drooping cedars, past the firs that stood silent in the silence of a world hushed by deep, dark green mosses. Pale owls flitted like ghosts among the trees; and, like ghosts, they made no sound in their passing.

Now, when Sea-Hawk reached the burial place, he could see the ghost bridge and the steaming, boiling ghost river that flowed under it without sound. He sat down at the edge of the gossamer world of ghosts. And a feeling of lightness came over him. The lightness rose in him, up, up, up out of his solid body. He felt himself float free of his solid body. He saw his body there, below him, while he, his spirit self, floated down to the gossamer bridge. He was there on the ghost bridge, all of him, looking much as he had looked before. But now he and his regalia and even his medicine rattle were made of some gossamer substance. He was paler than he had been and more luminous, yet not gray as the ghosts were gray. And he sensed that he was not cold, as the ghosts were cold – the ghosts he could see moving in the village across the ghost river.

He glanced back at the trees and at the moss in the graveyard. And again he saw that living, vibrating radiance that edged them. The world was more gloriously alive than most people suspected.

But not across the river. A soft owl's hoot drew him back to his purpose. He went over the bridge. And there the coldness touched him, the coldness of ghosts.

He saw faces he knew among the ghosts; and he cautioned them to silence. "Conceal me!" his hands said. And he slipped into the biggest of the gossamer houses unobserved by the chief of the ghosts.

There he found the filmy form of the old chief who had just died, vaguely diffuse, unsure yet of his new surroundings. And an eagerness leaped up in the ghostly eyes at the sight of the youth.

Again, Sea-Hawk cautioned silence. "Come with me!" he beckoned to the old man.

Ghost relatives glided around them as they fled to the ghost bridge and crossed it.

And there at the edge of the ghost river of boiling oil, there at the edge of the graveyard, Sea-Hawk slipped back into his solid body. "Now I will take you back to your body," he told the new ghost.

At once, the ghost contracted. The filmy substance concentrated itself into a small glow of energy, which Sea-Hawk grasped in his left hand and held safe as he fled back along the trail to the village.

The drums were still beating. The people were still singing as the shaman prince leaped triumphantly into the great cedar house.

The drums stopped. The singing stopped too. Even breathing seemed suspended as the youth dropped his cloak from his shoulders and glided toward the dead man's body, with his left hand high. Eagle down drifted away from his crown of grizzly-bear claws, and the puffin-bill fringe of his dancing apron clattered in the hushed house as he circled the fire four times. Then he swooped down on the dead man, opening his left hand on the silent body. "Eagle tail!" he commanded; and at once it was in his hand to fan the first breath of the old chief.

The dead man sat up.

The people gasped. Then they burst out into joyous shouts.

"The prince *is* a shaman," Little Wolf whispered. "The prince is a very great shaman."

The chief could only agree. Even without any training from the tribal medicine men, the prince was a very great shaman. And since the honor of his young clansman was close to his own honor, the chief said, "We will give Sea-Hawk a great medicine name at the potlatch . . . and install Raven's Wing as my true heir." Raven's Wing was a younger nephew.

"They must give me a very great name," Sea-Hawk insisted so forcibly that Little Wolf raised his eyebrows. Too much ambition was not good in a doctor.

But it was increasingly clear that Sea-Hawk was ambitious. It was as if he were determined to show that he could win more honor as a shaman than he could have won as head chief of a great tribe. Or as if the dream of being a medicine man had been dreamed so long that only exceptional success could make the reality as good as the dream had been. "Or," Little Wolf loyally suggested to his friends, "as if what he has already seen in the other world has excited him to push his powers to the limit. There is very great power in a very great name; so he wants it, to help him."

Others who were less fond of Sea-Hawk said that success had gone to his head.

Shamans, especially, glared at the boy who demanded a greater medicine name than any of them had. What infuriated them most was that he had accomplished his feat with their charms.

"If we had known you meant to be a shaman," they told him, "we would never have given you our most powerful charms when we brought you back to life."

"You did not bring me back to life," he corrected them. "For I had not died. My spirit self would have returned without your help."

"That may be true," Little Wolf pointed out to his friend. "But you are using their most potent charms."

". . . better than they would use them," Sea-Hawk pointed out in turn.

Little Wolf shook his head sadly.

"Little Wolf!" Sea-Hawk protested. "It's all coming out just as we planned! I'll be the greatest shaman in the world, and you'll all be lesser shamans. It's exactly as we planned."

It wasn't exactly as Little Wolf had planned. Instead of adventuring out to see the world as an eagle saw it or as a whale saw it, the shaman prince seemed to go only to the ghosts' village. And instead of curing the sick, he seemed to be more and more caught up in spectacular feats of bringing the dead back to life. There was his father's niece, then a man in another village, then a chief's favorite wife.

Thinking about the niece and the man and the chief's wife, Little Wolf felt his hair rise. Those three dead brought back to life were not quite like other people. Neither was the old chief brought back to life. There was something spooky about them. Something a little chill and gray. Something that made others edge away from them. They were ghoulish.

He talked to Sea-Hawk. But the shaman prince did not listen. In fact, he seemed scarcely aware of his old friend. His strangely wild eyes seemed to be burning right through Little Wolf and seeing far beyond him.

As the shaman prince brought more and more dead people back to life, no tribal medicine name seemed great enough for so gifted a young man to have. He came to be called simply Shaman Prince. And people paid him so lavishly for his work of restoring loved relatives to life that he became wealthy.

Yet, when these relatives were restored to life, people were not as happy as they had thought they would be. Little Wolf was aghast at the unease in the village as an increasing number of vague, grayish people haunted the gloomy corners of the great cedar houses. He tried to reason with his old friend. But Shaman Prince seemed obsessed with his own power.

Meanwhile, the ghosts across the invisible bridge were becoming very angry. Every new ghost that came to live with them was being cleverly snatched away before it had time to settle into the new life. And even happily settled ghosts were slipping away over the bridge, and hovering around villages until they found bodies to slip into. Other ghosts, agitated over the emptying of the great gossamer houses, kept stumbling into, or backing into, the ghostly River of Boiling Oil, thereby dying their second death and going on to their next phase, as Salmon People. Houses echoed with emptiness.

Finally, the chief of the ghosts called a war council in Ghost Town.

"Next time Shaman Prince comes here, we will cut off the end of the bridge," the war council agreed. "We will drop him into the River of Boiling Oil." That way, his spirit self would not linger in Ghost Town. Instead, it would be instantly routed on into the next phase. It would go to a Salmon Village to become the vital part of one of the Salmon People.

And to be sure that Shaman Prince would come again, soon, the war council sent a raiding party to his village that very night to snatch away a man's soul while he was sleeping.

In the morning, relatives found the man dead. And instead of chanting sadly as they would have done in the old days, instead of assuring one another that he was not really dead, but only gone to join other equally loving relatives in Ghost Town, everyone rushed to Shaman Prince. "He was not ready to die," they protested. "Bring him back to us, Shaman Prince!"

"He was not ready to die," Shaman Prince agreed. "The ghosts have taken him because they are plotting to kill me."

People gasped.

"Call the tribe together!" he commanded.

When the people were gathered, Shaman Prince commanded them to sing and sing and sing until he got back. "Sing all my songs!" he commanded. Then he glided away along the trail to the graveyard. And he was soon in Ghost Town.

This time, his ghost relatives edged away from him. But they made no move to stop him as he slipped into the chief of the ghosts' house and snatched up the soul of the newly dead man. In fact, it was only when he moved back toward the River of Boiling Oil, back toward the misty bridge with the man's soul, that the ghosts really seemed aware of their enemy's presence. Then they made a rush for him.

He leaped triumphantly onto the misty bridge, well ahead of his pursuers. And he was almost over it when it gave way beneath him. He made a frantic leap, landing so close to the bank of the real world that only his feet touched the ghost river. His gossamer body fell forward onto solid earth.

The soul escaping with him fell right into the river and disappeared in the boiling mists.

Groaning with pain, Shaman Prince pulled himself free of the river and re-entered his solid body. With superhuman resolve, he made himself run along the trail to the village. But before he reached the house where the people were still singing, he fell to the ground, groaning.

It was Little Wolf who sensed the groaning and slipped away from the singing, followed by his three friends. And the four youths carried their prince into the house. They laid him down on a plank covered with fresh cedar-bark mats.

The house hushed itself, and people's hearts sank. The great Shaman Prince would die, and no one would even try to bring him back because he had already partly died his second death. His feet had been burned in the terrible River of Boiling Oil.

He did not seem to see the people who gathered anxiously around him, nor hear faithful Little Wolf. Looking through people and beyond them, he listened only to his supernatural helper.

"Get up!" his power told him. "Run around the fire! Following the course of the sun, run four times around the fire!"

People gasped as they saw the prince rise on his horribly burned feet. They watched, open-mouthed, as he ran around the fire four times. Then they drew back in awe as they saw that his feet were both healed.

"Now I have more power than ever!" Shaman Prince called out. "Now I can bring back people who have been dead for many days."

Though Little Wolf protested again and again, Shaman Prince became more and more wild-eyed, more and more straggle-haired, more and more determined to empty Ghost

Town and fill the edges of the real world with increasingly ghoulish people. The stench of death began to blow through the village.

And across the river, the agitated ghosts were falling more and more often into the River of Boiling Oil, leaving the great gossamer houses more and more lonely.

Finally, the chief of the ghosts called another war council.

"We will give Shaman Prince a challenge he cannot resist," they agreed this time. "We'll say that the chief of the ghosts is sick and wishes the prince to save him from his second death."

By this time, Shaman Prince had so much power and so many supernatural helpers that he knew what the ghosts were planning. He even knew they intended to raid his village as soon as he had left it; they were going to snatch many souls of sleeping people to repopulate Ghost Town. So he called the tribe together and told them what would happen.

He also told them what to do. They were to mix certain poisons and evil-smelling things and sprinkle the mixture around the houses before they went to sleep. "Then, when the ghosts come in the night with their dried-nettle arrows, they will find that things happen differently than they expect."

At once, the people gathered the poisonous things and the evil-smelling things. But they did not sprinkle the mixture around the houses until two ghostly messengers had come for Shaman Prince in the night, and until he had gone off with them along the trail that twisted through dark, drooping cedars and past firs that stood silent in the silence of a world hushed by deep, deep, green mosses.

Confident of his own powers, the gossamer Shaman Prince went into the ghost chief's house. He calmly opened the filmy chest of ghost medicine regalia and took out the crown of dead-men's ribs. He shook out the dancing apron that clattered with a fringe of dead-men's bones. And he lifted up a rattle that was a skull, with a backbone for a handle.

Before he put on the crown of dead-men's ribs, though, he blew water into the hollow of his right hand and rubbed it on his forehead. Before he put on the apron that clattered with a fringe of dead-men's bones, he blew water into the hollow of his right hand again and rubbed it on his thighs. And before he shook the rattle that was a skull and backbone, he blew water yet again into the hollow of his right hand and rubbed it on both arms, while the supposedly sick chief of the ghosts scowled at him.

He was about to start work when he heard the hullabaloo outside. It was the raiding party, returned from the village.

"Our dried-nettle arrows failed us!" ghosts were complaining.

"Our arrows turned on us, killing some of us instead," ghosts were howling.

"Now we are fewer than ever," ghosts were wailing.

Shaman Prince heard no more. For his supernatural helpers were giving him instructions. "Run four times around the chief who pretends to be sick!" they were telling him. "Then kick the ground at his head! And jump back fast!"

Shaman Prince ran four times around the ghost chief. He kicked the ground. And, fortunately, he jumped back very fast. For the earth opened and swallowed up the chief of the ghosts.

The watching ghosts edged fearfully away from Shaman Prince. They did nothing to stop him from going back across the misty bridge, even though he took the ghost medicine regalia with him.

"I am the greatest shaman in the world!" he cried to his four friends when he got back to the village. "The greatest shaman who ever lived." Positively gloating in the crown of dead-men's ribs and the clattering fringe of human bones, he planned greater feats. There was no end to his ambition.

"You go too far, Sea-Hawk," Little Wolf told him; but he got no response.

The two were traveling together when they came to the place where a crowd of people stood weeping on a riverbank.

"What has happened?" Little Wolf asked.

"Our princess has drowned," they answered. "Our head chief's only daughter." And they pointed sadly to the river that raged along between its banks, swollen by the autumn rains.

"Find her body!" Shaman Prince commanded. "And I will bring her back to life."

It was spring before they found her. When they did, the princess was just a skeleton caught by a branch at the bank of the river. But they picked up the bones, laid them out carefully on a plank by the fire, and sent for Shaman Prince.

"You can't do this," Little Wolf told him. "She has been dead so long that she is happily settled in Ghost Town with her relatives, and with the young man who went over the bridge, too, while he was searching for her body. You can't bring her back."

"I can. And I will," Shaman Prince answered with flashing eyes. "Watch me!" And he started at once for her village.

Little Wolf watched the wild-eyed young man put on the gruesome crown of dead-men's ribs and the gruesome dancing apron that clattered with dead-men's bones. He watched him shake the skull and backbone rattle as he leaned an ear this way, and that way, to listen to his supernatural helpers. Then he watched him sprinkle warm ashes along the dead princess's bones four times.

And then he gasped. For the ashes had turned into flesh and skin.

But there was no life in the beautiful body.

Shaman Prince picked up his white eagle tail. The tribe seemed to hold its breath.

He fanned the cold flesh; and, suddenly, the princess breathed.

He had brought the princess back to life. Her grateful father lavished slaves on Shaman Prince, and canoes, and sea-otter robes, and costly coppers, and exquisitely carved mountain goat-horn spoons. . . .

But the gentle princess only looked about her in a vague, sad way. Then she turned yearning eyes toward Ghost Town, where her aunts and the young man who had gone over the bridge to be with her in the other world would be searching for her. And people edged away from her, though they did not know quite why.

"He has gone too far," Little Wolf said to his three other lifelong friends. "He is ruining life in the villages."

"He has gone too far," other shamans said to one another. No one was calling on them to cure a sick relative, with their powerful plants and their powerful songs and dances. He was ruining the profession of medicine. So they decided to trap him and kill him. They would invite him to a feast of shamans. And they would feed him a bit of dried human flesh—the most dangerous of all things to a doctor.

Shaman Prince received the invitation. And though his supernatural helpers warned him of what would happen, he decided to go. He would use the other shamans' jealousy to perform the greatest shamanistic feat the world had ever seen. He would die and bring himself back to life.

So he went to the feast of shamans. He ate the bit of dried human flesh. Then, at midnight, when he began to feel sick, he called in all his relatives. "The shamans have fed me dried human flesh," he said. And the people caught their breath before they turned to glare at all the other shamans.

"I am going to die," Shaman Prince went on. "But after I have been dead for a year, I will come back to life . . . if . . ." he glanced about him with his wild eyes, "if one of you will come and stand under my coffin to catch me." Now his voice thundered at them. "If you should fail to stand under my coffin and catch me, if you should be afraid of me, none of you shall be left. Now, who will volunteer to catch me?"

People shrank back. Shamans cowered. And Little Wolf clenched his fists and clamped his mouth shut. He would not help his old friend in this final madness.

"Who will volunteer to catch me?"

"I will catch you," a young voice called. And the people gasped.

It was Raven's Wing, the young prince who was heir now, in Sea-Hawk's place.

Sea-Hawk's eyes flashed. "My ghost medicine regalia!" he commanded; and his four lifelong friends brought it to him. When he had put on the crown of dead-men's ribs and the apron that clattered with a fringe of dead-men's bones, he ran around the fire four times, shaking his skull and backbone rattle. "Now. My coffin!" he commanded. And his four lifelong friends brought in a cedar box.

He lay down in it, still in his ghostly regalia. And he died at once.

People lit their torches and followed his coffin along the trail that twisted through the dark drooping cedars and past the firs that stood silent in the silence of a world hushed by deep, deep green mosses. They made a ring of flame around an empty grave tree and kept a terrified silence while the new coffin was hoisted up into the tree and secured there.

Raven's Wing shivered. He swallowed and licked his dry lips.

Little Wolf laid a hand on the boy's shoulder. "It will be a year before you must stand under the coffin," he reminded the young prince. "In the meantime, I and my friends will stand watch every night to see that no animal touches him. . . ." Or no angry ghost, he thought.

Night after night after night, Sea-Hawk's four faithful old friends stood watch, two by two, in the ghostly graveyard. And the year passed.

"It was a good year," Little Wolf said to his friends.

Many of the haunting gray people had gone back to Ghost Town. And no one had tried to restore them to life again. In fact, when another woman had died, her relatives had quickly comforted one another by saying, "She is not dead. She has just gone over the bridge and is being warmly welcomed by all the relatives who have gone before her."

"But the year is up tonight," Little Wolf added grimly. "And who knows what will happen if Sea-Hawk can bring himself back to life?"

The whole village was clearly as uneasy as Little Wolf was. And when evening came, many people slipped silently along the trail behind Raven's Wing.

Owls flitted like ghosts among the dark, drooping cedars and the shadowy fir trees; and, like ghosts, they made no sound in their passing.

The graveyard was chill and black with shadows. Mists wreathed among the grave trees and mortuary poles as though a tribe of ghosts, too, had come to see what was going to happen. People were silent.

Suddenly, there was a noise in the coffin.

Raven's Wing shuddered. And Little Wolf laid a firm hand on his shoulder. He urged the boy gently forward, toward the awful grave tree.

The coffin lid opened.

People gasped. Then they stood very still. All eyes were on the coffin.

A queer, warped, ugly owl flew out of the coffin and perched on its edge. It glared down at the gathered people with big, burning yellow eyes fixed immovably in their sockets.

A few people sank to the ground, terrified. Others pulled their blankets tightly about them to control their trembling. Little Wolf firmed his grasp on the boy's shoulder.

"I . . . I promised to catch him," Raven's Wing whispered, readying his arms as if to catch the fearsome bird. He edged closer to the grave tree. He was almost under the coffin when he dared to glance up into the awful, burning, immovable owl eyes. He stopped, terrified. And the owl swooped down at him with a blood-curdling shriek.

The boy sank to the ground, faint with fright.

The grotesque owl glided back up to perch again on the edge of the coffin. And now he spoke. In the voice of Shaman Prince.

"You were afraid of me. All of you. So not one of you will be left. Not one of the shamans who killed me. I will take all of you to Ghost Town, where I am chief now. The ghosts have made me their chief. You will all be my ghosts. And the shamans will be my slaves. For they killed me."

The queer, warped, ugly owl rotated its head to fix its awful eyes on everyone in the graveyard. "I will spare only the four friends who were my lifelong companions, the four friends who have kept faithful watch over me every night since I died. To them, I will leave my supernatural powers. And I will help them to become great shamans." With that, the queer, warped, ugly owl fell back into the coffin. And the lid fell shut.

The graveyard was chill and silent and black with shadows. Only the cold mists moved, wreathing away from the grave trees and the mortuary poles as if the ghosts were returning to their own land.

People looked fearfully at one another. Then, when nothing happened, they fled back along the trail to the village. Nothing happened.

The night passed, and the morning came. But still nothing happened.

"I am going to the burial ground," Little Wolf announced in a clear, firm voice; and he started along the trail. His three friends fell in silently behind him. And, one by one, other people crept along behind them. They stayed well back on the edges of the graveyard while Little Wolf climbed boldly up the grave tree, but their eyes were on him while he opened the coffin. They caught his surprised gasp and his look of astonishment. For there was nothing in the coffin except masses of eagle down.

"The sacred pledge of peace!" Little Wolf cried out to them, dipping his hands into the eagle down to waft it over the graveyard.

"Perhaps we will not die," people whispered to one another.

"Sooner or later we will all die," Little Wolf called out, as though he had heard them. He wafted more eagle down over the frightened people. "And some of us will die a second death in the River of Boiling Oil so that there will always be plenty of Salmon People, and plenty of salmon in the rivers." He blew yet more eagle down over them; and it drifted on them like soft snow. It clung to their dark hair as they made their way back along the trail that twisted through the dark, drooping cedars and past the firs that stood silent in the silence of a world hushed by deep, deep, green mosses.

Then the shamans began to die, one by one, the shamans who had killed Shaman Prince. And the four new young shamans told the people that the new chief of the ghosts had dropped his slave shamans into the River of Boiling Oil to let them move swiftly on into useful, exciting lives as Salmon People.

Then, one by one, people began to die, the people who had gone into the graveyard. But no one asked to have them restored to life. Instead, relatives comforted one another as they had in the old days. They said, "They're not dead. They've merely gone over the bridge to live with all the loving relatives who have gone there before them."

Little Wolf saw how the old ease came back to the village with the old acceptance of life and death. "And things go well now in Ghost Town," he assured the people. "Sea-Hawk is a great chief in that other world that has called to him all his life."

Then Raven's Wing died. And Little Wolf, remembering the valiant little fellow, brought him back to life at once with the help of the new ghost chief and the help of his three friends.

Word of this feat raced along the river. And when a prince died in another village, the new chief there sent for the four young shamans. He offered them slaves and canoes and sea-otter robes and costly coppers and carved food chests and exquisitely carved mountain goat-horn spoons if they would restore the prince to life.

"Your prince has been dead four days," Little Wolf protested when they reached the sorrowing village. "And the new chief of the ghosts has forbidden us to restore life to anyone who has been dead for four days." He turned sadly away and went back to his own village to work over a sick woman.

But the three other young medicine men lingered, tempted by the slaves and canoes and sea-otter robes and costly coppers and carved food chests and exquisitely carved mountain goat-horn spoons.

"He is scarcely over the four days," they told one another. The odor of death had scarcely touched his body. "We'll bring his soul back to his body," they told the sorrowing chief.

And when they had ordered the people to sing and sing, and beat on the hollow cedar planks and on the skin drums, they lay down near the dead prince and went into a trance. Their souls left their bodies to go to Ghost Town to find the soul of the dead prince.

Instead, they found the chief of the ghosts. He was waiting for his old friends in front of the great, gossamer house where the new young ghost was being cared for by ghost aunts and ghost uncles and fond old grandfathers and grandmothers.

"You have a bad smell," the Ghost Chief said, waving the three young shamans angrily away from him. "So I know that you have disobeyed my orders about the four days. You will not return to your people. You will stay here with me now."

Back in the sorrowing chief's house, the people sang and sang and sang. They beat and beat and beat on the hollow cedar planks and on the skin drums. But nothing happened. The souls of the three young medicine men did not come back to their bodies. By and by, their three hearts stopped beating, as the prince's heart had stopped. So the chief sent for Little Wolf.

"Take your prince to your burial ground," Little Wolf told the sorrowing chief. "Set the emblems of your family like a fort around him. And remember that he is not really dead. He has merely gone on to the land of ghosts to live with all the loving relatives who have gone there before him."

The chief and his people did this.

And hearts grew easy again in the villages all along the river.

"The laws of life are good," people said to one another.

Acknowledgements

"Householder" from *Telling the Tale* by Robin Skelton © 1987 Porcupine's Quill Inc. Used by permission of Robin Skelton.

"The Phantom Dog Team" from *Green Woods and Blue Waters* by Harry Paddon. Used by permission of Breakwater Books.

"Conversations With the Little Table" from *High Spirits* by Robertson Davies. Copyright © Robertson Davies 1982. Reprinted by permission of Penguin Books Canada Limited.

"Shoeless Joe Jackson Comes to Iowa" by W. P. Kinsella is reprinted from *Shoeless Joe Jackson Comes to Iowa* by permission of Oberon Press.

"Buggam Grange: A Good Old Ghost Story" from *Laugh with Leacock* by Stephen Leacock. Used by permission of the Canadian Publishers, McClelland and Stewart, Toronto.

"Up North" from *Home Truths* by Mavis Gallant © 1981. Used by permission of Macmillan of Canada, a Division of Canada Publishing Corporation.

ACKNOWLEDGEMENTS

"The Snow Walker" from *The Snow Walker* by Farley Mowat. Used by permission of the Canadian Publishers, McClelland and Stewart, Toronto.

"The Timeless Island" from *The Timeless Island and Other Stories* by H. R. Percy © 1960 The Ryerson Press. Used by permission of H. R. Percy.

"The Ghost Hunter" from *Tales from the Igloo* by Father Maurice Metayer © 1972 Hurtig Publishers. Used by permission of the Missionary Oblates.

"Ghosts Have Warm Hands" from *Ghosts Have Warm Hands* by William R. Bird © 1968 Clarke, Irwin & Co. Ltd. Used by permission of General Publishing Co. Ltd.

"The Mackenzie River Ghost" from *Trail and Campfire Stories* by Julia M. Seton © 1940. Used by permission of Estate of Julia M. Seton.

"Kismet" by Johann Polberg is used by permission of the author.

"Ghost Story" from *Once More Upon a Totem* by Christie Harris. Used by permission of the Canadian Publishers, McClelland and Stewart, Toronto.

Contributors

Robin Skelton is the author, compiler, or editor of more than sixty books. He is also the founding chairman of the creative writing department at the University of Victoria and a co-founder of the *Malahat Review*.

Harry Paddon grew up in Labrador, where he spent much of his adult life working as a trapper. Today, he lives and writes in British Columbia. "The Phantom Dog Team" originally appeared in *Atlantic Advocate* magazine. It is also included in *Green Woods and Blue Waters*, a collection of Paddon's stories.

Robertson Davies was Master of Massey College in the University of Toronto for twenty years. He has also written numerous books, including *Fifth Business*, *World of Wonders*, and *What's Bred in the Bone*. In 1975 he won the Governor General's Award for fiction.

W. P. Kinsella is the author of, among other books, *The Iowa Baseball Confederacy*, *The Moccasin Telegraph*, and *The Thrill of the Grass*. *The Fencepost Chronicles* won the 1986 Stephen Leacock Medal for humour.

Stephen Leacock, Canada's most renowned humourist, was born in 1869 in England, but immigrated to this country as a child. His nearly forty books include

Sunshine Sketches of a Little Town, Arcadian Adventures with the Idle Rich, and *Moonbeams from the Larger Lunacy.*

Mavis Gallant was born in Montreal, but left Canada in 1950 to live in Paris. A regular contributor to the *New Yorker*–"Up North" originally appeared there–she is the author of ten books, including *Overhead in a Balloon, The End of the World and Other Stories,* and *Home Truths,* for which she won the Governor General's Award for fiction in 1981.

Farley Mowat's more than two dozen books include *People of the Deer, Never Cry Wolf, The Boat Who Wouldn't Float,* and *My Discovery of America.* He has won numerous awards for his writing, including the Governor General's Award and half a dozen honourary doctorates.

H. R. Percy, a former member of the Royal Canadian Navy, was born in England. He is the author of several books, including *Flotsam, Tranter's Tree, A Model Lover,* and *Painted Ladies.* He was also founding chairman of the Writers' Federation of Nova Scotia.

Father Maurice Metayer was born in France but spent most of his life, as a member of the Oblate Order, serving in the Canadian Arctic. He also wrote several books on Inuit mythology and linguistics, among them *Arlock l'Eskimau, Tradition Esquimaude,* and *I, Nuligak.*

Will R. Bird was born in Nova Scotia and served with the 42nd Royal Highlanders of Canada during World War I. His many books include *The Shy Yorkshireman, So Much to Record, Angel Cove,* and *Off Trail in Nova Scotia.*

Julia Seton was the wife of Ernest Thompson Seton. In addition to *Trail and Campfire Stories,* her books include *American Indian Arts: A Way of Life* and *By a Thousand*

Fires: nature notes and extracts from the life and unpublished journals of Ernest Thompson Seton.

Johann Polberg is a potter, poet, and short story writer living in North Vancouver. Her work has been published in several journals and two anthologies. She is a member of the Federation of British Columbia Writers and the Canadian Poetry Association.

Christie Harris lives in Vancouver. She is the author of numerous books, including *You Have to Draw the Line Somewhere, Confessions of a Toe-Hanger,* and *Let X Be Excitement.* Her book *Raven's Cry* won the Book of the Year Award from the Canadian Library Association.

